D1824712

AN IMPOSSIBLE LOVE

A SINGLE DADDY ROMANCE COLLECTION

MICHELLE LOVE

HOT AND STEAMY ROMANCE

CONTENTS

Made in "The United States" by:

Michelle Love

© Copyright 2021

ISBN: 978-1-64808-127-9

ALL RIGHTS RESERVED. No part of this publication may be reproduced or
transmitted in any form whatsoever, electronic, or mechanical, including
photocopying, recording, or by any informational storage or retrieval system without
express written, dated and signed permission from the author

❧ Created with Vellum

ABOUT THE AUTHOR

Mrs. Love writes about smart, sexy women and the hot alpha billionaires who love them. She has found her own happily ever after with her dream husband and adorable 6 and 2 year old kids. Currently, Michelle is hard at work on the next book in the series, and trying to stay off the Internet.
"Thank you for supporting an indie author. Anything you can do, whether it be writing a review, or even simply telling a fellow reader that you enjoyed this. Thanks

.

BLURB

When a constitutional crisis means the resignation of the President of the United States, Independent Congressman Orin Bennett is suddenly elevated to the highest office in the land. Young Secret Service agent Emerson 'Emmy' Sati is thrust into the political world when she becomes both the youngest and the only female agent assigned to protect the bachelor President.

Trying their best to stay professional, it soon becomes clear that Orin and Emmy are attracted to each other, but with political and personal enemies snapping at their heels and both of their careers on the line, can they ever be together?

During a week at Camp David, they give in to their attraction, and afterwards, they continue the illicit affair in the White House, knowing that with every meeting, they risk discovery, the consequences of which could prove disastrous for both of them. Romance seems to be only a pipe dream for both Emmy and Orin, and when death threats are sent to the new president, Emmy must remain professional at all times—or risk losing Orin in the worst possible way.

CHAPTER ONE

Three a.m.
   Washington DC
   Inauguration Day

Emerson Sati rolled over in bed, groaning at her alarm clock. Who the hell gets up this early? She turned onto her back and tried to blink herself awake. The Big Day. Inauguration. And in a few hours, American's third bachelor president—and only the second one to win office as an Independent after George Washington—would be sworn in, and she, Emerson Sati, Special Agent, would be standing by, waiting to take a bullet for him.

She slid out of bed in her tiny apartment in Georgetown and padded to the shower. At four-thirty a.m., President-Elect Orin Bennett would be ready to go for his usual morning run along the Washington Mall and on the path that ran alongside the Potomac, and she would have to run beside him. Not that she minded—it got the exercise for the day out of the way so she could concentrate on her work. Just... why the hell did he have to get up so damn early?

The hot water helped, and she massaged shampoo through her long dark brown hair. I need a haircut, she thought while drying it. It fell almost to her waist now, and she had to resort to ever more elaborate hairstyles to keep it neat and tidy. She glared at her reflection in the mirror. She knew people regarded her as beautiful, but Emmy couldn't care less. She wasn't in her job because she was good looking. She was the first female agent to protect the president—selected personally by him after he consulted her boss. If Emmy had still had her family around, they would have been proud. Zach had been proud.

Of course, Zach would have been proud if she breathed in and out. He had been her partner in the Secret Service, pure business at first, but she soon learned that underneath the gruff exterior, he was the kindest, most brilliant man she had ever met. They had never let their love interfere with their work, but it was obvious to all how crazy they were about each other. Zach had wanted her to do well in the Service; he had transferred to Virginia right before their wedding and was tasked with protecting the then-Congressman Bennett's campaign manager, Kevin McKee. Three days before Emmy would have become his wife, Zach was shot and killed by a man with mental health difficulties who wanted to 'punish' McKee for some random crime he thought the young politico had committed.

He might as well have put a bullet in Emmy's heart as well. She was in shock, broken, and full of rage. Her boss Lucas, head of the presidential detail, had told her to take a sabbatical.

"Take it or you're out of here, Emmy, and you know that's the last thing I want for you." His voice had been kind but firm.

She'd fought him, of course, but her need to grieve for Zach overtook everything. She went to India, her dad's homeland, and spent time trying to find peace. Everywhere she went she saw Zach: his dark blonde hair, choppy and messy when not working; his dark blue eyes twinkling with merriment and love for her.

Eventually, real life crept back in, and her need to return to her work overwhelmed the grief. Lucas had welcomed her back, delighted to find that her passion for work was still as intense as it had been before Zach's death.

In his office that November day, as the rest of America still reeled from the shock of the impeachment, Lucas told her about her new role.

"Obviously, we can't have the same agents protecting President-Elect Bennett who protected former President Ellis. President Ellis's entire team is now under investigation by the FBI, so we have to assume that they have all been compromised." Lucas smiled at her. "President-Elect Bennett handpicked his new team. You were the first person to be selected."

"I was?" Emmy looked astonished. "I'm honored."

"But?"

"President-Elect is what? Six-foot-five?"

"And change."

"And I'm five-five. He knows that, right?"

Lucas grinned. "Em, you've proved over and over that height doesn't matter. With your record, why should Bennett care?"

"What's he like?"

Lucas considered. "A good man. A little bewildered that he made it to the Oval Office. I don't think anyone expected that, least of all him. He said he was running simply to make a point about having a fresh start outside of partisan politics, but I think he underestimated the country's thirst for honesty."

"Sing it, brother," Emmy rolled her eyes. "I've never questioned my country more than in the last few months—not that it affects my commitment to the job," she added hurriedly, and Lucas laughed.

"Em, don't worry. I don't figure you for a dissident. One thing," he said, meeting her eye. "You know as well as I do that Orin Bennett is fiercely loyal to his team, and he has a small but select group of people he trusts implicitly. Kevin McKee is one of them. I know that your personal life has nothing to do with your job, but still, I have to ask the question."

Emmy had anticipated this. "Sir, I have no ill feelings or resentment towards Mr. McKee. He was no more to blame for Zach's death than anyone else. The man who killed Zach was sick, and I cannot imagine what hell he was and is going through."

Lucas was impressed. "You are one hell of an agent, Emmy. The very best."

Emmy thought about her boss's words as she drove through predawn Washington DC. No, she would never waver from the commitment she had made five years ago when she joined the Service, but like her countrymen, she had been shocked by the scandal that brought down the Ellis government and elected an Independent congressman from Oregon to the highest office in the land.

Brookes Ellis, once revered as a forward-thinking, inclusive Progressive, had betrayed his voters when it came to light that he was using the office of the president to further his own agenda and had spent millions of dollars of taxpayers' money to do so. And when some of his minions had been found guilty of human trafficking, Ellis's incumbency was ruined, even though he strenuously denied any links to such atrocity.

Ellis hadn't gone quietly and was still railing against the system and the new president. Just yesterday, he had gone on The Today Show to besmirch the fact that President-Elect Bennett was an Independent, the first since George Washington.

It wasn't Emmy's job to get involved with the politics, but she knew there were a lot of disgruntled Ellis voters, some of whom were vocal about their desire to see Bennett dead. Always the crazies, Emmy thought now as she parked her car.

She made her way to Blair House, the traditional home of the president-elect, on Pennsylvania Avenue. As she showed her ID to the security there—a matter of protocol only because they knew her well—she went to change into her running gear.

As she liaised with her fellow agents, President-Elect Bennett came to meet them. He grinned at them all. "Ready, folks?" He smiled at Emmy. "What do you say, Agent Sati? Maybe ten kilometers today?"

Emmy smiled. "Whatever you say, sir."

Emmy had to admit, there was no downside to watching Orin Bennett exercise. His tall frame was broad and his shoulders and arms thickly muscled. A former Nasa astronaut and Marine, Orin Bennett was in his mid-forties and ripped like she'd never seen. The man looked as if he'd been hewn from rock. How the hell was he still single?

Emmy berated herself. She had a job to do—God help her if Bennett took a bullet because she was busy objectifying the man. But there it was—Orin Bennett was hot as hell.

After forty-five minutes of brisk pacing, Bennett signaled he'd had enough, and they escorted him back to Blair House. "Good run, folks, thank you." He grinned at Emmy again. "You kicked our butts again, Agent Sati."

"That's my job, sir," Emmy shot back with a wicked smile. Bennett chuckled.

"You heard the woman, guys. Better behave yourselves."

"Good luck today, sir," Emmy said suddenly, then flushed red. Orin smiled.

"Thanks, Emerson." It was the first time he'd called her by her first name, and she felt a thrill zing through her. His light olive-green eyes crinkled at the edges as he smiled. "You, too."

Her fellow agent Duke nudged her as they walked back to the field office changing rooms. "Think the almost-pres is sweet on you, Boo."

Emmy frowned at him. "Don't say that out loud again, Duke, please. It's hard enough being a woman in this job without people spreading rumors."

Duke gave her a smile. "Sorry. It's true, though. Okay, okay, I'm sorry," he added hurriedly as she raised a tightly clenched fist and pretended to punch his face.

Emmy couldn't really blame Duke for what he said. Orin Bennett had made a point of being friendly toward her since she'd joined his team, and at first, it seemed as if he were making a point about her gender and her youth. But yes, after a while, she had begun to think it might be something else, which was flattering... but completely unrealistic. In fact, she might be tasked to be close enough to take a bullet for him, but there was no man farther away from her on the planet.

Seven hours later, as Emmy watched Bennett take the oath of office, her eyes raked the area constantly for threats with her instincts set on high. Like every other American who had grown tired of the corruption and the absence of humanity in the last government, she felt proud. Soon enough, Orin Bennett would face his critics—and there were already many of them—but today, he stood tall. His speech might not have made history like Kennedy's or Obama's, but it spoke of a new dawn over the American landscape, one of hope and inclusion.

At that moment, Emerson Sati knew she was protecting one of the good guys, and it made her heart swell with pride.

Orin Bennett, newly minted President of the United States, stood behind the "Resolute desk" and looked at his small team of trusted advisors.

Charlie Hope—his old friend from NASA, now his national security advisor.

Moxie Chatelaine—the firebrand from New Orleans, who had run his campaign for president. The proud African-American woman was now his chief of staff.

Peyton Hunt—who'd begun her career as a comedy writer for a popular Eighties TV show before moving into politics. America's first female vice president.

Kevin McKee and Issa Graham—his communications director and press secretary, respectively.

These were the five people who had fought every inch of the way to make him—goofy old Orin Bennett, space cowboy and military grunt—the freakin' President. He grinned at them now.

"Relax, everybody. I just have one question... what the hell just happened?"

He grinned widely and sat down as they broke into relieved laughter. Orin put his hands flat on the desk. "Can you believe they've left me charge of this thing?"

"Honestly?" Charlie Hope shook his head. "No way, dude. What are they thinking?"

Orin grinned as his friends joined in. "Insane."

"The country's gone mad."

Orin sat back, laughing. "You realize I could have you all recommissioned to Lagos?"

"At least it would be warm," Peyton rolled her eyes as she sat down on one of the striped couches. "What was it today? Twenty degrees?"

"Blame FDR, not me. Okay so... what now? Clock's ticking on our first one hundred days, and I don't want it all to be about picking out soft furnishings and pranking former staffers. Well, not all about that, I'm just saying." Orin was having trouble taking all the pomp and ceremony seriously, but he was also anxious to get to work. America was broken by scandal, and he wanted the process of healing to begin.

As Moxie and Kevin went through the rest of the week's schedule, Orin flicked his eyes over to the small dark-haired woman standing silently in the corner of the room.

Agent Emerson Sati. The most beautiful woman he had ever seen. When her boss had come to talk with him about his protection, Lucas Harper had pushed for Emerson to be included on Bennett's detail, regaling Orin with a glowing appraisal of her career and work ethic.

Orin had simply no reason to turn her down; he wanted an inclusive, open team of both men and women, after all. He'd agreed and then a couple of days later, Lucas brought Emerson to meet the president-elect. As soon as she'd stepped into the room, Orin knew he had made a mistake.

There was no way he'd let this woman take a bullet for him. Her caramel skin was set off by the darkest brown hair tucked up into an efficient bun at the back of her head and the deepest brown eyes he'd ever seem. Add in a rosebud mouth and a body that still retained its curves even as it was athletic, and Orin was lost. He knew nothing could ever happen between them, especially now that he was president, but, God, if he'd met her before...

What are you thinking, idiot? You're the President of the United

States, not some schoolboy with a crush... but spending time with Emmy, especially on their early morning runs, wasn't helping.

He dragged his attention back to the room. Moxie was talking about the opening salvos of their administration.

"Of course, what everyone wants to know is... will you pardon former President Ellis?"

Orin sighed. "I haven't made my decision on that yet. I don't feel as if I have enough information about what he knew or didn't know."

Kevin McKee, a blue-eyed dark-haired Princeton graduate, snorted. "He knew everything, Orin... sorry, Mr. President. Brookes Ellis was corrupt even way before he was elected."

"Well, we know that, but the American public will want proof. They're shell-shocked—reeling." Orin leaned forward. "Who's that guy, the pit bull, the one who always shut down any threat—Ellis's damage control?"

"Martin Karlsson?" Charlie Hope looked doubtful. "Weasel."

"Agreed but useful. We need to get him in here and let him think we're considering a pardon. Maybe he'll talk."

"He might refuse to come. He's made some pretty inflammatory remarks about you to the press."

Orin shrugged. "I want us to make it a policy to not respond to petty bitching. He, or anyone else, says anything defamatory, that's a different matter. The country comes first here; that's what we have to always keep at the top of our agenda. Too many people are on the bread line, or in need of medical help for us to waste time on petty minutiae, agreed?"

The others murmured their assent. "Talking of minutiae," Issa Graham, the press secretary spoke up with a grin, "InStyle magazine wants to know what you're wearing for the balls this evening."

Orin rolled his eyes. "Heels and a mini-skirt," he grinned. "Tube top." He sneaked a look at Emerson Sati as the others laughed and was gratified to see her lips twitch.

"Can you imagine the reaction?"

Orin snorted. "After the last President, anything goes, Issa. Now, what's next?"

CHAPTER TWO

Duke whistled at Emmy as she walked toward him wearing the dark red dress that clung to her curves. Her chestnut hair was down for once, swept over a shoulder, and she actually had makeup on—not much, but enough to enhance her natural beauty. She shot him a look, and he grinned. "Sorry, I know it's not appropriate, but dang, girl, you look amazing."

Emmy flushed despite her disapproval. "Thanks, man. You don't want to know where my weapon is." She regretted her words as soon as they came out of her mouth as Duke grinned widely. "Shut up, Dukey," she said, smiling and shaking her head.

"Shutting up."

They were walking through the West Wing towards the Oval.

"Lucas say what time the president would be ready?"

"Any minute. Ready for dancing?"

Emmy rolled her eyes. "Yeah, because we'll be doing a lot of that."

"You wearing that dress? Anyone who doesn't know you're on the pres's detail will be clamoring for a dance. Wait, I didn't even see that thing from the back." Duke looked approvingly at the backless dress.

Emmy sighed. "Yeah, nor did I when I grabbed it from the rack. Do you think it's inappropriate?"

Duke shook his head. "Not at all, but now I really want to know where your weapon is."

Emmy grinned. She didn't mind Duke's playful flirting. He had been one of Zach's best friends in the Service, and he was married to Emmy's best friend, Alice, another agent. Their jokey flirtatious friendship didn't mean that either of them wouldn't take a bullet for the other. They were family.

Lucas met them in the outer office of the Oval. Jessica, the president's secretary, a spritely woman in her sixties, nodded approvingly at Emmy's outfit. "Nice. Good to see you dressed like a girl for once."

Emmy smiled at her. Jessica Fields was legendary within Bennett's circle, a mentor to him when he was a young congressman, and now his aide-de-camp whenever he needed a critical eye. "You can go in, folks."

Duke led the way, and Emmy could hear Orin Bennett talking to his cohort. As she walked into the room, he glanced over at her, and his voice faltered. He gazed at her for a long moment, then looked down and went on with what he was saying. Emmy could feel her face burning but she said nothing and just took up her usual post against the wall. Moxie Chatelaine grinned at her, and with a tiny nod, indicated her dress and mouthed Wow at her. Moxie herself looked incredible. Her long dreadlocks were piled elegantly on top of her head, and she wore a gold dress which glowed against her dark skin. Emmy nodded and smiled, and then kept her expression neutral as she looked around the room at the handsome men and the stately women all ready to celebrate this most unlikely election victory.

Orin was dressed in a dark grey suit, exquisitely tailored by the finest Italian designers. Emmy may not have had the money to buy the designer gown she was wearing—luckily the agency paid for it— but she knew quality.

But it wasn't the suit that made Orin Bennett look so... devastating. Much had been made in the press of the bachelor president's incredible good looks—the more salacious press continually speculating on who he was sleeping with.

Emmy knew he had been in a long-term relationship with a woman a few years previously, but, yes, at the moment, he was resolutely single. The press didn't know what to make of his reticence to discuss his love life, not accepting his "I just want to concentrate on healing the country" line.

There were five official inaugural balls for this president; Bennett insisting to the Presidential Inauguration Committee that he wanted no more than five and to make the tickets for each cheap enough for members of charities to attend. That directive hadn't gone over well with the two main parties desperate to start lobbying the Independent president.

His date for the balls would be the widowed vice-president, Peyton Hunt. Their friendship made it easier for them to enjoy the evening, but it also waylaid any gossip about who they would bring. Of course, it didn't stop people talking about the two of them as a couple either, but they both figured that would be the lesser of all evils. Their decades-long friendship from way back in college was well known, and Peyton's late husband, Joseph, had been a good friend of Bennett's, too.

Emmy, assigned to the evening's detail, would attend all the balls as well—the president wasn't expected to spend very long at any one function, just enough time to thank his campaign staff and supporters, and to network with politicos from The Hill. Food and drink were supplied in plenty, but Emmy knew from old that the president wouldn't get to enjoy any of it.

Nor would she or any other of the president's security, and now her stomach growled at the thought of food. Emmy wasn't one to ever deny herself culinary pleasures; in fact, she was known within the detail as having a huge appetite. Many a time she'd been challenged by Zach to a hot dog-eating competition; he hadn't stood a chance and he loved that about her.

"Nothin' worse than a woman who picks at her food."

Emmy grinned at the memory, then forced herself to focus. As they walked into the first of the events, the Youth Inaugural Ball held at the Hilton, Emmy scanned the invited guests.

Because of the importance of this day, her boss Lucas, the head of the presidential security detail was present and close to the President's side at all times. Emmy, Duke, and the other agents were all at their stations, their movements all rehearsed until they were second nature. With one scan of the room, Emmy noted where the president was, where his political rivals were, and where the entrances and exits to the room were. The hotel had been scoured for explosive devices and every guest was thoroughly vetted by the FBI. Nothing was left unchecked. It was a routine job as far as they were concerned, but they were still on high alert. A liberal president had a lot of enemies, especially from the previous administration.

Emmy saw former President Ellis' national security advisor Steve Jonas—one of the few cabinet members who had been totally exonerated in the investigation. She knew President Bennett was hoping he would stay on to assist Charlie Hope, but as of yet Steve Jonas hadn't made a commitment. No one knew where his loyalty lay.

"Em, come in." Duke's voice boomed through her ear piece, and she winced a little.

"Yeah, Duke. What's up?"

"Just checking in. Nothing to worry about so far."

"Jonas is here. Not that I'm saying that's something to worry about, but you know. Just in case."

"Gotcha." He chuckled softly. "Only four more of these."

"Yup." She gave him a quick smile as she spotted him across the hotel ballroom. She knew Duke found these kind of close scrutiny jobs dull, but she loved them, loved trying to work out the psychology of people's body language. She saw the Senate leader approaching President Bennett. Robert Runcorn had been a close ally of Brookes Ellis until the scandal broke, then he quickly dumped his connection to him. A weasel, Runcorn nevertheless wanted Bennett to pardon Ellis and had been very vocal about it in the press.

Orin sighed inwardly as he saw Rob Runcorn approach from out of the corner of his eye. Orin had been enjoying talking to the invited guests, particularly some young people who had served their communities and were inspirations to their peers. He really didn't want Runcorn to interrupt them with yet another passive aggressive rant about Brookes Ellis. Orin saw Emerson Sati watching Runcorn, too, and felt a rush of gratitude. If Runcorn got too forceful, he knew she would step in.

And Goddamn did she look beautiful in that red dress. Her long, almost black, hair fell in soft waves beyond her shoulders, and her body in that dress was...

"Mr. President? May I have a moment of your time?" Damn it. He'd lost focus, and now Rob Runcorn had seen an opportunity.

"Of course, Rob, always a pleasure," Orin said smoothly. He shook the other man's hand while studying him. Prematurely aged, Runcorn was only in his late fifties but looked a decade older. Too many good dinners and port, Orin guessed, but nevertheless, he stepped away from the group he'd been speaking to with an apologetic smile. "What can I help you with, Bob?" Like I don't know.

"I know this may not be the most appropriate place to speak with you about this, but... Brookes Ellis."

Orin sighed inwardly. "Bob, you're right, this isn't the time or the place. Can't we just enjoy tonight without mention of former President Ellis?"

"You know it'll be the first thing we bring to the table in your administration."

"I do know, and look, I'll be ready and willing to listen to what you have to say. What both parties have to say. But, Bob, I must warn you. I don't take these allegations lightly. There will be no soft soaping of the investigation, and if there is even a hint of President Ellis being involved, he will have to face the consequences."

Runcorn's face was significantly less friendly after Orin had finished speaking. With a sneer on his face, he gave Orin a humorless smile. "Well, we'll just have to see how that investigation pans out." He looked around the room and saw Emerson lurking beside them, listening to their conversation. He knew she was a Secret Service agent.

"Tell me, President Bennett, what was your criteria when choosing your detail? Ability to look good on the job?"

Orin's smiled vanished. "Bob, if you have something to say, say it. My personal detail is none of your business, but I'll say this. The agents chosen were selected for their outstanding service. Most of them are former military. Tell me, Bob, did you serve?" He knew full well that Bob Runcorn had never stepped foot on a military base in his life, let alone been on the front line.

Bob muttered something that sounded like a sarcastic "Congratulations, Mr. President" and moved away.

Orin met Emerson's gaze. "Don't pay any attention to him, Emmy. He's a jerk."

Emerson flushed. "Thank you, Mr. President."

"Have you eaten anything?"

Emerson shook her head, glancing around the room. She wasn't supposed to be talking to him, but she couldn't exactly ignore the President if he wanted to talk.

"No, sir. Not while I'm on duty." She gave him a quick smile but tried to communicate to him that she would get in trouble for not focusing. Orin seemed to understand her silent plea.

"Well, you're all doing a great job, Agent Sati. Carry on."

"Yes, sir."

He touched her arm then moved away to talk to some more of his invited guests, and Emmy sighed with relief. After Duke's comments earlier, she felt more than a little paranoid about her colleagues wondering if the president was playing favorites.

That was the stuff of fantasy, she told herself, and she should not fantasize about him while she was trying to protect him. Besides, she barely knew the man. He might turn out to be one of those sleazy guys who thought every woman he saw was his personal property—not uncommon in men of power. There must be a reason he never married.

Emmy pushed these thoughts away, and the evening progressed. The president attended all the official balls, and even some of the unofficial ones, delighting a coterie of elderly charity mavens as his presence lit up their small gathering.

Emmy saw Lucas visibly relax the further they got toward midnight. She knew his work ethic sometimes caused him significant stress—which he didn't show—but she'd learned how to read her boss and mentor. She shot him a quick smile as she passed, tailing the president as he finally began saying his goodnights.

The team escorted Bennett back to the White House and at last, their relief took over. Before he went to the Lincoln bedroom, he thanked them. "Great job today, guys. Thank you all."

He winked at Emmy who nodded, hiding a smile. "Thank you, Mr. President."

"Seriously, when you're off duty, please call me Orin."

"Yes, Mr. President," Emmy shot back immediately, and they all laughed. Orin held up a hand.

"Fair enough. Goodnight, all."

"Goodnight, sir, and congratulations."

As beautiful as the dress was, Emmy was relieved to change out of it and into her leggings and a sweatshirt. She was starving, but until the debrief concluded, she still had a job to do.

Thankfully, Lucas didn't keep them long. "I just want to say thank you. With countless people unhappy about this president, we had no right to expect today would go off this easily, but it did. Tomorrow we begin the real work, but for tonight—" he glanced up at the clock and smiled, "or for the rest of this morning, I should say, get some rest."

"Get some food," Duke muttered, and they all laughed. Lucas nodded.

"That, too. The kitchen here has left some cold cuts out for anyone who needs them, but I say Ben's Chili?"

"Hell yes."

Emmy decided not to go with them, despite Duke's pleading. It had been Zach's favorite place, and she hadn't gone back there since his death.

"I'm fine, honestly," she smiled at him. "I'm bushed. I have to be back on duty at seven, so I'm going to grab a sandwich and bed down in one of the staffrooms."

They couldn't persuade her otherwise and eventually gave up. Emmy wandered down to the White House kitchen, her stomach rumbling. She saw not just cold cuts but a whole counter full of food —fresh salad platters, meats, fresh baked bread. She grabbed a plate and loaded it, piling potato salad alongside creamy pasta and a pile of pastrami and sat down on a stool to enjoy it.

She was just shoving a huge forkful into her mouth when she heard his voice.

"Is it as delicious as it looks?"

Emmy choked as she shot to her feet, and she had to cover her mouth to swallow. "Mr. President," she mumbled.

Orin smiled at her. "At ease, Agent. Finish your food."

Emmy chewed quickly and swallowed too big a mouthful.

"Excuse me, Mr. President, I didn't expect anyone else to be down here."

"Don't tell anyone, but I'm ravenous," he said with a smile and took a plate. He studied hers. "Nice combination you've got there, Agent Sati... may I call you Emmy now that your off duty?"

"Of course, Mr. President."

He chuckled and lowered his voice. "And while we're alone, you can call me Orin, Emmy."

"Afraid I can't, sir. Protocol."

Orin stood, pretending to consider. "Okay then, how about I order you to call me Orin?"

Emmy felt awkward, but also was aware of a thrill running through her body. "Mr. Pres..."

"That's an order, Agent, from your Commander in Chief." He was obviously enjoying teasing her.

Emmy suddenly smiled. "Whatever you say... President Orin."

He threw his head back and laughed, then loaded his plate and sat down opposite her. "What a day, huh?"

"Yes, sir."

"Emmy."

"Yes... Orin."

"That's better." He shoved a forkful of food into his mouth and indicated her plate. "Eat up."

They ate in companionable silence for a few minutes, and Emmy was aware of his scrutiny. She met his gaze finally. His green eyes were soft.

"I wanted to say how sorry I was to hear about Zach. I didn't know him personally, but Kevin McKee is alive because of Zach's sacrifice, and I can only honor his memory by saying he died protecting a good man."

Emmy felt her throat close. "Thank you, Mr—Orin."

He smiled at her, holding her gaze a beat too long. She was amazed to see two spots of pink appear high on his razor-like cheekbones.

"Well," he said, getting to his feet, waving her back down as she stood with him. "Thank you for your company, Agent Sati. I'd better take my food and go check my e-mails. Big job starts in the morning."

"Yes, sir. And congratulations, Mr. President."

"Thank you, Emerson. Goodnight."

"Goodnight, sir."

CHAPTER THREE

Orin would soon discover that as leader of the free world, that there was plenty to distract him from the fantasy of bedding Emerson Sati. The matter of the former president's pardon was the first question lobbed from the gaggle of journalists at his first press briefing as president.

"Obviously, it's something I'm going to have to consider if—and that's a big if—the investigation finds no wrongdoing on President Ellis's part. But, folks, I want to caution you against playing judge, jury, and executioner. I think we all feel that the former president's resignation speaks volumes, so let's all wait for the investigation to come to a conclusion. Yes, Kathy?"

Kathy Mills, The Washington Post's veteran journo, stood. She smiled at Orin. "Sir, can we ask what your personal feelings on this matter are?"

Orin smiled. "I'm waiting for the investigation's findings, Kathy. Do I think there was some—how should I put this—lack of integrity on the former administration's part? Yes. Again though, people make mistakes, and whether there were any nefarious reasons for it, we shall see. Until then, I won't be making any decisions. Thanks, Kathy. Mark?"

Mark Woolley from The Wall Street Journal stood. He looked a little uncomfortable. "Mr. President, as you well know, you are the first president to take office while unmarried. There's obvious speculation. Could you confirm whether you are actively seeking a, um, romantic partner?"

"Mark, you look embarrassed to be asking that question."

The press corps laughed, and Woolley nodded sheepishly. "I am, sir, yes."

Orin grinned and shook his head. "Nothing to tell. I'm concentrating on the country, and the first one hundred days."

After the press briefing, Moxie met Orin as he walked back to the Oval. "That went well."

"They were throwing me softballs," he said, "I know these people. Next time, it'll be like having open heart surgery without the anesthetic. What's next?"

"Charlie and his frat bros."

"Mox, is that any way to talk about the joint chiefs?" Orin chuckled. "Hey, Jessie."

His secretary smiled at him. "Commander Hope and his colleagues are waiting, sir."

"Thanks, Jess." He saw his security detail change over, and Emerson Sati followed him and Moxie into the Oval Office. He nodded hello at her and was rewarded by her quiet "Good morning, sir." Christ. She was so beautiful. He dragged his focus back to the meeting at hand and asked Charlie to brief him.

Emmy spent the next few days focusing solely on the job of protecting the president. She had to think of him almost as a god, not as a man, or she'd think about Orin the man, and the fact that he was devastatingly charming. She even laughed at her little crush. It was never going to happen.

Three weeks into Bennett's tenure in the White House, and Lucas called the detail into a meeting with the FBI.

"We have the first real credible threat against the president," he told them. "We had the usual bunch before and after inauguration—crazies typing crap on message boards and hiding behind their keyboards. Today, however, we received intel that a small group of Brookes Ellis's supporters have gone rogue."

"We're taking his fans seriously?" Duke sounded incredulous, and Emmy understood why. The former president's fanbase was furious that he'd been forced to resign, but their anger was impotent at best. With President Bennett an Independent, there wasn't the usual partisan furor, and their legs had been taken out from under them with his election.

"We are. We're talking far-right fanatics here. They don't want a progressive candidate behind the 'Resolute desk'." Lucas flicked some images up onto the screen. "Meet Max Neal, leader of the Justice for Brookes Ellis campaign."

There was a murmur of derision.

"Justice?" Emmy's voice was dry and sarcastic, and Lucas smiled.

"Well, exactly. Anyway, this young man is from old money—Connecticut money—Ellis's home state and I'll give you one guess who his college roommate was."

Emmy raised her hand. "Looking at his age, it's got to be Martin Karlsson."

"Bingo." A picture of Ellis's former advisor filled the screen. "And as you all know, Mr. Karlsson is due to visit the Oval Office later today, so I'm assigning three extra agents. Emmy, Duke, you'll be in the Oval. Jake, Mike, in the outer office. I need you to listen to his language, watch his attitude, pick up on anything you find strange. When he arrives, Duke, I want you to escort from the front gate, and when he leaves, Emmy, you escort him back. He doesn't spend one second inside the White House without an escort, understand? Even if that means following him into the restrooms. He won't like it but screw him."

"Sir?"

"Yes, Em?"

"Is the President aware of our concerns?"

"I'm briefing him after the meeting."

"Do we really think he would attack the president in the Oval?" Mike, one of the other agents spoke up.

Lucas shook his head. "No, of course not. This assignment is about watching and listening. I want to know everything Karlsson says and everything he hears while he's in the White House."

After he dismissed them, he called Emmy back. "Hey, kiddo, come walk with me."

Outside, he smiled at her. "Been hearing good things about you from the president's staff."

"Thank you, sir."

Lucas chewed his lip. "Also heard some gossip, and I wanted to check in with you that it was just gossip."

Emmy felt her stomach drop. God, no. Had someone overheard Duke teasing her? Or seen her talking with Orin after the inauguration and made more of it than it was? "Sir?"

"There's a rumor going around that the president... God, how do I put this? That the president is dating the vice president."

Emmy felt relief washing over her. "Sir, as far as I know that's not true. The vice president is, I believe, still in mourning for her husband."

"You understand why I'm asking. Both the president and the vice president like you very much, Emmy, and if they were going to conduct a relationship within the White House, they'd need their detail on their side, so..."

"Understood, sir, but as I say, nothing to report."

As Emmy made her way back into the White House, she felt nothing but relief. Ever since Inauguration, she had been worried about the consequences of that private moment she shared with the president, scared someone had seen them and drawn the wrong conclusion, or that the president had confided in one of his aides. What had she been thinking? She had worked so hard for this job and lost so much for it that she couldn't risk it for a man she could never have. Zach had given his life to protect the president's right-hand man—how could she dishonor his memory like that? She shook her head. Get over yourself, Sati. All that happened was a cute back-and-forth tease, nothing else.

Later, as she waited with the president in the Oval, they were alone for a few minutes as Duke escorted Martin Karlsson into the White House.

Orin smiled at her. "Agent Sati, I wanted to say... I'm sorry if our little chat the other night made you uncomfortable. It was unfair to you and unprofessional of me. I'm sorry."

"No need to apologize, Mr. President," she said, trying to keep her voice calm and steady. "But thank you anyway."

Orin smiled, and opened his mouth to say something else, before shaking his head. "You're a good agent, Emmy. Don't let anyone ever tell you otherwise."

"Thank you, sir."

A knock at the door and Jessica announced Martin Karlsson. The man followed her in, accompanied by Duke. Karlsson didn't look happy that he had been 'escorted' through the building and shot Duke an unhappy glare. Duke kept his face smooth. Karlsson's eyes flicked to Emmy, appraising her body. Emmy was used to it and gazed back at him unflinching. She knew he was in his late thirties and single, completely devoted to his cause.

Orin offered Karlsson his hand. "Mr. Karlsson, good morning."

"Thank you for seeing me, Mr. President. I appreciate your time."

"I appreciate yours," Orin said smoothly, "Please, let's sit and talk."

Jessica closed the door as she left the office. Karlsson sat when offered a chair, and Orin sat opposite him. There was a noticeable difference in height between the two men; the president towered over his guest at six-foot-five. Emmy kept her eyes on Karlsson. He would have been checked at the gate, so she knew he had no weapons, but still, her job was to make absolutely sure he was no threat.

Martin Karlsson had bright blue eyes which twitched from side to side. If she had to guess, Emmy would say he was a coke user, probably using it to fuel the energy to work twenty-four hours a day. The guy looked exhausted.

"Mr. President, thank you for seeing me. As you know, I'm here to make my case for a Presidential pardon for former President Ellis."

"Getting right down to business, Martin?"

The other man smiled. "Just my opening salvo, Mr. President."

Emmy listened to their conversation which went as expected: Karlsson made his case, Orin heard him out and then gave him the same answer he gave the press. It clearly dissatisfied Karlsson, but he was magnanimous.

"I understand, Mr. President." He stood and shook the President's hand. "This is just the first of many conversations, I promise you."

"I'd expect nothing else. Keep in touch with my office, Martin. Anything we can tell you about the investigation, you have my word, we'll share it."

"I appreciate that, Mr. President."

Emmy escorted Karlsson back to the lobby. They didn't speak, but he did nod politely to her as he left. Emmy had to admit that he was more impressive than she had first thought: passionate about his cause and loyal—if inadvisably so—to Brookes Ellis.

She reported as much back to Lucas. "Sir, I don't think we have to worry about Karlsson. I think the threat would be more insidious; Karlsson wears his heart on his sleeve too much."

"Thanks, Emmy, great work."

Off-duty, Emmy changed clothes and then drove to the Secret Service gym in Laurel and worked out for a couple of hours. She ignored the admiring glances of her fellow male agents and rolled her eyes along with her female colleagues, used to the unguarded admiration of the surrounding men. They were used to being objectified, the only saving grace being that while on duty, the men kept their baser thoughts to themselves. It was annoying but part of being a woman in this business.

And like the rest of the female race, Emmy couldn't help but compare her petite, curvy body to the lithe, taller agents around her.

She knew her Indian heritage had a lot to do with her breakneck curves that, no matter how hard she worked out, stayed soft and fleshy, rather than trim and athletic. Luckily, her curves belied the fact that she was a kick-ass athlete—despite her loathing of running —and expert level in Muay Thai, but even she found the constant workouts a drag. Part of the job, Sati, she told herself as she went through her routine. After this, she would drive back to her small apartment in Georgetown and finally get some downtime.

Two hours later and she was in her car, windows down even on a cold February day in DC. The fresh, sharp air woke her up, and she felt invigorated and ready to.... what? What did she have to do? Her friends were all in the Service and either redeployed to other parts of the world, on duty, or catching up on sleep. She had toyed with getting a dog after Zach had died, something to help her cope, but her long hours and time away wouldn't be fair on the mutt. Still, as she opened the door to her apartment, it rang with silence, and Emmy imagined a sweet little furball coming to greet her.

"Hey, Missy Moo."

Emmy smiled and turned to see her elderly neighbor, Marge Johnson, waving at her from her door across the hallway.

"Hey Margie Moo, how are you? I'm sorry I haven't been by for a couple of days. Work, you know?"

"Of course, dear, protecting that handsome man. Lucky girl." Marge was in her nineties, a sassy lady who still highlighted what she wanted to watch in the TV Guide and spent her days playing the piano and singing songs about her 'sweethearts.' She also had a pretty serious Coca-Cola habit, enjoying at least one little glass bottle a day; she would often ask Emmy to come join her for an hour or two, which Emmy did gladly. They would sit out on the old woman's deck and either talk or just relax in a companionable silence. Marge was the closest thing Emmy had to a parent, and she loved the older lady.

"Listen, some guy came by to see you... well, he said to see Zach. I didn't tell him anything, obviously, but I took his name and number. Missy Moo, you wouldn't believe it if I told you, but he was the spitting image of your Zach. A little taller, a little scruffier, but just like him."

Emmy felt a jolt of pain shoot through her heart, and she had to look away from Marge's gaze. She studied the piece of paper. All it said was his name—Tim—and his phone number. "Did he say who he was?"

Marge shook her head. "He didn't say. Does Zach have a family? Brothers?"

"Not that I was aware of, but his family was pretty fractured. His mom left the family early, and his dad kicked him out when he was young. Maybe he could have a half-brother or a cousin... I just don't know." Emmy chewed her lip. "And you didn't tell him Zach is dead?"

Marge shook her head. "I didn't think it was my place to, lovely girl. Was I right?"

Emmy hugged her. "Thank you, Marge, you did great. I'll call this dude and see what's happening."

"Want to come in for a Coke?"

Emmy smiled but shook her head. "No, I have stuff to do, but thanks, Moo."

"Alrighty, you know where I am."

As Marge tuned to go back into her apartment, Emmy called out to her. "I've been thinking about getting a dog, Moo."

"I think that's a wonderful idea," Marge beamed. "I could look after it while you were at work."

"You sure?"

"Of course! I had dogs all my life up until a few years ago. My Eva keeps telling me I'm too old, but what does she know?"

Emmy grinned at her friend. "Then you should come with me to choose him or her at the shelter."

"Just let me know when and where, Moo, and I'll be there."

Emmy went into her apartment feeling lifted and happy. She would get a dog and with Marge's help, maybe some of the loneliness would abate. She dumped her workout clothes into the washer and went to change the sheets on her bed. Doing chores relaxed her, gave her time to think, and she cleaned the whole apartment. When she was done, she showered, then put a pan of water on the stove to boil for pasta. She put some fresh salmon into the steamer and while it was cooking, she toyed with the idea of calling 'Tim.' Something in her held back though; did she really want to deal with this? Lately it had felt like she was turning a corner in her life; that although the pain of Zach's death would never leave her, it had simmered down to a dull ache instead of the raging agony.

She tucked the name and number behind a magnet on the fridge and pushed it to the back of her mind. When her supper was cooked, she flicked on the television. More news about her boss. Alone at home, Emmy could watch Orin Bennett; as the television news showed the latest news along with old b-roll footage of when he was a Congressman and footage from the Inauguration, she could appreciate the man rather than the president. Onscreen were scenes from one of the balls, and Emmy felt herself color when she saw that the President had been watching her as he talked to some of the guests. Please, God, don't let Lucas see this. If her boss thought an attraction on either side was building between Emmy and Bennett, she would be shipped off to the Nebraska field office before she could say 'schoolgirl crush.'

But still, when she went to sleep that night, she dreamed of pressing her naked body against the president's hard chest, feeling his arms around her and his lips against hers.

CHAPTER FOUR

Lucas thanked Jessica when she told him the president was ready to see him and knocked on the door to the Oval.

"Come on in, Lucas. No need to knock." Orin Bennett waved him into a seat. "Moxie tells me you have some updates for me?"

"Yes, Mr. President. I'm afraid I don't have good news. The far-right group led by Max Neal has splintered into separate groups, and our intelligence tells us they are planning... something. Domestic terrorism, an attempt on your life—at the moment, we're hearing different reports. We'll pin down more details today, but I must ask you this. Are you still planning on going to Camp David this weekend?"

"I am. The FBI director is coming with us, and we're going through the evidence they have collated about former President Ellis." Orin sighed. "Look, I don't really care about the threats to my life—it comes with the territory. But I want every available threat to the general public investigated and thwarted. Every one of them, Lucas. We need to contain this situation before it spirals."

"Of course, Mr. President, but may I ask you a question? Cancel Camp David. Hold the meetings here. It's already leaked that you're intending to go to Camp David and—"

"And the place would have already been swept and locked down. Lucas, I appreciate your concerns and I trust your judgement, but we're going to Camp David."

Later, Orin retired to his private study and sat heavily down on the couch, a stack of papers on the coffee table in front of him. Lucas's warnings were at the front of his mind, not necessarily the threats to himself, but he couldn't stand it if his enemies targeted innocent people. The last thing America needed was another terrorist attack, mass shooting, or bombing.

Orin knew all about disaster. He and Charlie had been in Mission Control when the Columbia space shuttle exploded upon re-entering the Earth's atmosphere. He remembered the hopeless call of CAPCOM asking repeatedly for the shuttle's crew to respond, knowing they never would.

Columbia, Houston, UHF comm check. Columbia, Houston, UHF comm check...

The disbelief. The flight director's tears, then the efficient, numbed contingency procedure, the one all NASA employees hoped they would never have to use. It had been shattering.

Orin had left the space program after that, Charlie following him three years later. Charlie re-enlisted to serve in Afghanistan for two tours, then quit to marry his childhood sweetheart, Lynn.

Orin, determined to assuage the helplessness he'd felt watching the Columbia crew die, made the move into politics. Moving from mayor of Portland to the House of Congress representing Oregon, all on an Independent ticket. The American public was tired of partisan politics, and Orin soon found himself the new political darling of Washington DC. The media were taken by surprise, having underestimated the country's thirst for honesty.

Brookes Ellis's impeachment only exacerbated that thirst; Orin was elected in a landslide, and the country waited for a new dawn.

Orin loved his country, loved to serve them, and was ready to take on the mantle of President, even when sometimes he couldn't quite believe he was in the Oval.

And yet... sometimes the loneliness got to him. His last relationship—with a human rights lawyer, Sophie—had ended four years ago.

"I love you," Sophie had told him, "but I can't be your consolation prize, Orin. You need to serve your country, and that doesn't leave time for me. So, I'm out."

They had parted on amicable terms, and even hooked up a couple of times since, but now Sophie was married to a hot-shot Manhattan lawyer and had a kid on the way.

Orin tackled a couple of the memos on his table, then took his glasses off, rubbing the bridge of his nose. Just once, he'd like to chat with a partner, someone with a common connection other than work or shared history. Someone new. His mind drifted to Emerson Sati again, and he chuckled and shook his head. The trouble it would cause to start something up with one of his protective detail... he couldn't imagine; the press would have a field day.

Ever the strategist, he amused himself by working out how they could make it work. They'd need someone on the inside to help them...

"Cool your boots, cowboy." He had no idea if Emmy even liked him in that way. Even sharing a moment that night in the White House kitchen... he didn't know her well enough to know whether she had been humoring him during their back and forth or if it was indicative of something more.

Plus, the poor kid had lost her fiancé in the worst way. And he would resign himself to leave her alone before he screwed up her career. No. Emerson Sati was off limits.

Orin got up and wandered down to the kitchen again, telling himself he was just looking for a late-night snack, but when he entered the kitchen the place was deserted. When he heard the clip-clip of high heels, his adrenaline surged only to die when Moxie, his chief of staff, entered the room.

She grinned at him. "Hey, dude."

"Hey, Mox."

Off-duty, his old college friend Moxie was the one person who didn't always refer to him as 'Mr. President.' She headed for the freezer now and hefted a liter of ice cream out. "I've been sitting in my office dreaming of this all day." She grabbed two spoons and nodded at the bar stools. "Sit and share with me."

"What flavor?"

"Duh. Pistachio, of course."

They spooned some of the dessert into their mouths, and Moxie moaned in pleasure. "God, this takes me back. Remember when we used to stuff ourselves with this, staying up all night to finish term papers?"

"God, yes." Orin grinned at her. "Those were the days."

"Indeed. We stayed up all night, eating ice cream, sharing joints, and now look where we are." Moxie laughed, her chuckle deep and throaty.

"Your momma always said weed was a gateway drug. Guess she just didn't mean the White House gates."

Moxie grinned, then studied him. "You look like you have something on your mind, O. Spill it."

Orin smiled, but hesitated. "You get lonely, Mox?"

"Sometimes, I guess. Actually, I've been seeing this poly-sci post-grad for a few weeks. Nothing serious, but I like her. What's up, O, you need me to get you some girls?"

"Best wing-woman ever."

"I'm serious. You know we could arrange for..."

Orin rolled his eyes. "God, Mox, I'm not looking to get laid. I'm just beginning to think there might be more than just work."

"Hallelujah, he sees the light at last." Moxie grinned at him, then gave him a questioning look. "Anyone in the running?"

He shook his head. "No one I can have." He got up and washed his spoon off, drying it on a dishcloth. Years of single life had made him good at housework. He was about to put it away when the next words out of Moxie's mouth made him freeze.

"Agent Sati?"

Orin turned to face his friend, his expression tense. "Is it that obvious?"

"Only to me, but I have known you half your life. She's gorgeous, Orin, and a sweet girl."

Orin nodded. "Ha, girl. Exactly. She's half my age and my protection detail. Is there anyone on Earth less available to me?"

Moxie pretended to consider. "The Queen?"

Orin grinned, pretended to look affronted. "You think the Queen wouldn't want to get with this?" He pulled a bodybuilder's pose to make her laugh, and Moxie covered her eyes.

"I will never un-see that now. When you're talking to the Russian president or the ambassador to the Federated States of Micronesia, I'll look at you and just see that." She giggled as he made an even more ridiculous pose.

"Just called me Fabio."

A small cough behind him made him start, and he looked around to see Emmy Sati trying to hide a grin. "Mr. President."

Moxie chuckled. "You missed the worst of it, Em. Really."

Orin felt both embarrassed and absurdly pleased to see Emmy. He loved that shy smile, the pink blush in her cheeks. "Good evening, Agent. You get the graveyard shift tonight?"

"Yes, sir."

"I won't blame you if you fall asleep." God, his small talk needed work. Moxie obviously thought so, too, given the massive eye roll she gave him. She hopped off her stool.

"Well, I'll say goodnight, folks." With a wave, she was gone, shooting Orin a meaningful look that he couldn't figure out. Was she encouraging him or warning him off?

Orin watched as Emmy spoke into her earpiece. "I'm with Eagle, check."

"Copy that, Em."

"Always vigilant." Orin smiled down at her. God, the curve of her bottom lip. He wished he could trace it with his finger, pressed his own lips to it. He was aware he was staring, but he couldn't look away. Her eyes were so big, such a warm brown surrounded by thick black lashes, devoid of makeup; they made his stomach quiver.

Emmy looked away, and he realized once again that he was out of

Line. "Say," he said lightly, "Walk me back to the Rose Garden, would you? I could do with some fresh air."

"Of course, Mr. President."

They walked through the White House and to the Rose Garden. Outside, it was freezing, but neither mentioned it. "Tell me something about yourself, Agent Sati."

She hesitated. "Well, sir, I was thinking about getting a dog."

"Well, that's exciting. You know, the president usually has a White House dog. Maybe I should follow your lead."

"Maybe, sir. I'm hoping to adopt one from a shelter."

"Good choice." He pondered a while. "What sort of dog do you think I should get, Agent?"

He watched as she hid a grin. "An Afghan hound, sir." She shot him a sideways look. "With that flowing blonde hair... you could call him Fabio."

For a moment, Orin didn't realize she was teasing him. Then he grinned at her. "Touché, Agent Sati."

He saw her shiver a little but immediately try to hide it. "Let's go in," he said, placing a hand on her back briefly, "I keep forgetting how cold it is."

"Isn't the weather inclement in Oregon, sir?"

"It can be, Pacific Northwest and all that, but DC winters? Jeez, Emerson. They take some getting used to."

"Indeed, Mr. President."

"Are you from the DC area, Agent?"

Emmy shook her head. "No, sir, New Orleans."

"Ah, Nawlins. Ugh, forgive my terrible accent." He gave her a sheepish smile.

Emmy grinned. "All is forgiven, sir." They were at the entrance to the private residence now.

"Are you coming to Camp David, Agent Sati?"

She shook her head, and he felt a rush of disappointment. "No, sir. Duke and Greg are your detail for the trip." She gave him a rueful smile. "I've been told to use my vacation time up, sir, or I'd be there."

"No, no, you deserve a break. Anything planned?" Please don't say you're spending time with another man...

"Only to find a dog, sir."

"Well, good luck with that."

Emmy smiled. "Thank you, sir, and have a good trip to Camp David."

As Orin went to bed, he thought about his reaction earlier. Please don't say you're spending time with another man... "Just how damn selfish are you, man? She deserves some happiness after what she's been through." Orin shook his head, berating himself. Just because you're so damn lonely...

No. He had to get his mind away from Emerson Sati. Maybe he would ask Moxie to set him up with some women—just dating, nothing major. Kevin would know some people. The suave communications director, all blue-eyed charm and dashing good looks was never short of a date. Post-grad students, human rights lawyers, political lobbyists—Kevin had the market on strategic dating. Power dating. Orin smirked. Kevin also had all the confidence his looks, background, and job awarded him.

As Orin washed his hands, and splashed water on his face, he looked in the mirror. "And you're the President of the United States," he told himself. But he still felt like that country boy from Oregon.

He lay in bed trying to sleep but instead he thought about Emmy's soft beauty, those pink lips curving up in a smile, or open in a gasp as he made love to her. "Goddamn it," he growled and turned over, blocking the thoughts from his head.

CHAPTER FIVE

Emmy and Marge saw him at the same time. The white fur, the big brown eyes, the one ear cocked, the other bent over. "Oh, yeah," Emmy breathed as she knelt down by the cage. "This is him."

"He's so beautiful," Marge looked like she might cry, and the shelter assistant looked vaguely bemused. The dog, a mix-breed, was not what anyone else would call 'beautiful,' but he had a raggedy charm. The assistant opened the cage, and the dog slid out, wary, but sniffed Emmy's hand and allowed her to stroke him.

"Hey, boy..." Emmy felt a surge of affection as the little dog jumped up and put his paws on her knees, sniffing at her face. "What's his name?"

"We actually don't know. He was a stray, but we've been calling him Major. Despite his appearance he does have something about him, something a little—"

"Regal," Emmy nodded. "Hey, Major."

Major licked her face, and she giggled. She picked him up and cuddled him.

Marge scratched his ears, and he panted happily, almost looking as if he were smiling. "Yes, this is your boy," she said to Emmy, and Emmy nodded, her mood lifted just being in the presence of this adorable little mutt. The adoption process would take a couple of weeks, but she knew she was making the right decision.

As she drove Marge and herself home, Emmy thought about the chat with the president. She liked his sense of humor; when she'd walked in on him posing ridiculously to make Moxie laugh, she'd had to bite back a hysterical laugh. Goofy. The President was a goofball.

At home, she sat with Marge for an hour before the other women fell asleep. Emmy covered her with a blanket before letting herself out. Looking around her apartment, she imagined Major curled up on her couch or eating from a bowl on the kitchen floor. She'd let him sleep on the bed with her; that was a no brainer for Emmy. She could see it now, curled up together on her couch while she read or watched movies. She couldn't wait for him to come home.

In the kitchen, she grabbed some cold pizza from the fridge, then noticed the phone number she had been ignoring for days now. Tim. 555-6354.

Tim. Tim, who looked so much like Zach that Marge had been beside herself.

Zach had never talked about his family except to say he wasn't close to them. It was another thing he and Emmy had in common— they were each other's family, along with Marge and their friends in the Service, and that was good enough for them.

She pulled the piece of paper off of the fridge, then jumped as someone knocked on her door. Would Tim have decided to come try again, seeing as no one had called him back? Emmy steeled herself for that and went to answer the door.

She relaxed when she saw Moxie Chatelaine outside. "Hey, Mox." The chief of staff had sometimes been to Emmy's house; the two women had become friends when they were off-duty. Moxie was still flanked by two of Emmy's colleagues, however, who still performed the appropriate 'apartment sweep' before Moxie and Emmy were allowed to be alone.

Emmy made them both coffee. "This is a nice surprise. I thought you'd be on your way to Camp David."

Moxie grinned at her, thanking her for the hot drink. "Oh, I am, but I just wanted to come see you and get your read on a situation."

"That you couldn't run past Lucas?" Emmy was surprised, and Moxie shook her head.

"It's, um, a little sensitive. It's..." Moxie sighed. "Oh, I'm just going to say it. It's about the President... and you."

Emmy felt her face burn, and she looked away from Moxie's searching glance. "I don't understand."

"The blush says you do. He likes you, Emmy."

Emmy took a sip of too-hot coffee, feeling it burn her throat. "Mox... I swear, I haven't done anything to encourage anything, I haven't broken any protocols—"

"Girl, chill. This isn't a conversation about POTUS, me being CoS, or you being an Agent. It's about me, Moxie, being friends with two people who are obviously attracted to one another."

Emmy shook her head. "We should not be having this conversation, Moxie, please."

Moxie reached out and took her hand. "Orin isn't someone who sleeps around; he doesn't get involved with many people. He's charming and funny, but rarely if ever have I seen the way his face lights up when you're near. And, girl, don't lie. You like him, too. This is just me, Em, your friend, in your apartment. Nothing leaves this room, I swear."

"You know what it would cost me if this ever got out... and hell, there's nothing to get out. But even a whiff of partiality on my or the president's part, and my career is toast. I'll be shipped off to somewhere, and I'll never see him again."

"I know. I know the cost. I also know the hell you've been through." Moxie was silent for a long time. "But, Em, when two people like each other, it's a damn tragedy if they can't at least give it a go."

Emmy gave a humorless laugh. "Now I know you're insane. It can never happen, Mox. I'm the President's protective detail. I can't sneak into the Lincoln bedroom while I'm trying to protect him."

"There are ways we could make it work."

"Lucas would actually kill me dead. With extra deadness."

Moxie laughed. "Which is why you need someone on the inside to help you. I'm not saying anything; I'm not being your pimp. Why not come to Camp David with me? Have dinner one-on-one with Orin."

"Actually insane." Emmy felt irked now. What the hell did Moxie think she was playing at?

"He's lonely, Em. I offered to get dates for him, but he's only interested in one woman."

"This isn't fair, Moxie. I feel like... God, if I say no, will I be shunted out of my job? Is this an executive order?" Emmy's eyes filled with tears, the panic setting in.

Moxie got up and put her arms around Emmy. "Stop. I'm sorry. I'm sorry. I didn't know it would upset you this much. Of course, we can forget it. I'm sorry. I was just... God, I don't know... trying to matchmake two people I love."

"I'm his agent, Mox. You know as well as I do that it's an impossible situation. He can't go anywhere in the world without scrutiny, and I have a job to do. I take that job very, very seriously. Come on now, you know how hard I had to work to be the first female on his detail, let alone the first Indian agent to protect the President."

Moxie sat back down. "Can I ask?"

"What?"

"Do you like him?"

Emmy busied herself. "I voted for him, if that's what you mean."

Moxie rolled her eyes. "Em."

"Fine. Yes, he's very attractive; yes, I'm human after all. But crushing on the President of the United States isn't reality, Mox. Please, can we drop this?"

"Of course, Em. Listen, you got some time off?"

Emmy nodded, still disturbed by the strange conversation. "I'm getting a dog."

"Huh."

"What?"

"Oh, nothing," Moxie had a mischievous grin on her face, "Just that Orin was talking about getting a dog earlier. Coincidence?"

"Yes." But now Emmy found herself grinning. "Dogs will save the world."

"Amen to that."

Moxie stayed a little while longer, then left for Camp David. Emmy switched the lamps on in her apartment and scooched down on the couch. She deliberately flicked the television to a loud action movie, but it didn't distract her the way she wanted it to.

Moxie had set something off in her brain—the fantasy, the dream of being close to Orin Bennett. Emmy couldn't deny that she had been excited when Mox told her that he liked her. God, this was just like ninth grade... except with nuclear buttons and service issue sidearms.

The thought of spending time with Orin, just as Emmy and Orin, was like chocolate to a diabetic—rich, delicious and mouthwatering —but entirely off limits.

The movie started to get on her nerves, and she shut the television off and lay down, staring up at the ceiling. Since Zach had died, she hadn't been with anyone else—hadn't been attracted to anyone else—but she had to admit to the heat she felt inside her when she was with the president, and if she was honest, she knew he was attracted to her, too. You couldn't fake that chemistry, she thought.

There are ways we could make it work...

Damn it, Mox, why did you have to tell me that? Because now, all she could think of was kissing Orin Bennett, sliding her hands under one of his expensive Italian shirts, letting her fingers move over the ripple of his stomach muscles, cupping his cock through his pants. Damn.

She wondered what it would feel like to be underneath him, gazing into his eyes as his cock thrust into her. Emmy gave a moan and slid her hand between her legs, rubbing her clit through her jeans as she fantasized about Orin Bennett making love to her. She stroked herself into a mellow orgasm, and then closed her eyes. She wanted to call Moxie on her cell phone, an unsecured line, and say the words which could start the ball rolling on something no one could control. She wanted to say the words but forced herself not to.

So, how do we make this work?

Emmy sighed and rolled off the couch and headed to the shower, cranking the water to run cool in an attempt to jolt herself out of the fantasy.

Max Neal, far-right-wing activist, placed the photographs out on the large table in the farmhouse's kitchen. In the middle of rural Pennsylvania, he and his small group of trusted colleagues had come to strategize and regroup. Max had realized early on that he was the focus of the Secret Service and FBI as soon as Orin Bennett had been sworn in, and so he disbanded his group to go underground.

There were six of them now, and he, Max, was the only one among them who had spent time as a mercenary. He didn't really understand why they were following him, a rich boy from old Virginia money, but he'd take it. He loathed the new president, and he had been disappointed when his old college roommate, Martin Karlsson, had chosen to distance himself from Max. Traitor. He was looking forward to ruining Martin's life as well as removing Bennett from office.

He looked around at his assembled cohort now. "Break time is over. Our opening move is nearly here, and we have to be prepared to back it up with real action."

One of the mercenaries, a rail-thin but athletic man named Steve, nodded at him. "Everything's set—they might see it coming, but that's the point. If they think we're disorganized, they might take their eye off the prize. Certainly, they won't expect who we're targeting—this time."

Max smiled. "Which leads me to this." He went to the board they'd set up and pinned five of the six photographs onto. "The people protecting Bennett. Lucas Harper is the head of the Presidential detail. He leads a small team dedicated to protecting the President, normal stuff. These are his agents: Duke Hill, Gregory Stein, Walker Lamb, Jordon Klee." He pointed out each man and then waved at the last photo. "And then there's this agent."

He pinned the last photograph up on the board, and the men whistled and hooted. Max smiled. "Yup. Agent Emerson Sati. Steve, I believe you've already crossed paths with the lovely lady?"

Steve grinned. "Yeah, her fiancé got in the way of the bullet I meant for Kevin McKee. Tragedy."

"Especially for the lovely Ms. Sati. Not that she's a pushover herself. Recruited straight from Harvard where she graduated summa and at the top of her class in training at Rowley. Don't be fooled by her pretty face, she's lethal. However—"

He turned his laptop around and pressed play on a video he'd cued up. "Take a look. See anything interesting?"

He watched them as they viewed the video. It showed President Bennett's Inauguration Ball. One of them, at least. Karl, one of the mercenaries whistled. "Damn, that girl is hot." Max looked at the screen. It showed Emerson Sati in a dark red, backless dress, protecting the president.

"You're not the only one who thinks so. See anyone else admiring the little beauty?"

He watched their faces as they studied the video then Steve cackled with laughter. "Well, looky-loo. The pres has a crush on his protection?"

Max grinned. "That's my read. Which makes Agent Sati our number one concern. If they're fucking, she's going to be distracted."

"That's not likely though, is it?"

Max shrugged. "Who knows? The President of the United States can have just about anyone he wants." He glanced at the video, grinning lasciviously. "And he wants."

They all chuckled, then Max closed his laptop. "So, these are the six people we need to watch closely. I need you to report every move they make. I want to know if they use the bathroom, where they get their groceries, who they hang out with. Everything."

He tapped Emmy's photo again. "And I want to know if she is screwing Bennett. If she is... she'll be key to our getting to him."

"And if she gets in our way?"

Max smiled coldly. "If Bennett is as crazy about her as I think he is... he'll be devastated when she takes a bullet for him."

CHAPTER SIX

"You said what?"

Moxie grinned at her old friend as they sat together in Aspen Lodge, the presidential cabin at Camp David. She had just told him what she and Emmy Sati had talked about, and now Orin looked bemused and a little horrified. Moxie chuckled. "I just told her that there are ways."

"Oh for God's sake, Mox." He stood up and paced, then turned to her. "What did she say?"

Moxie's smile was victorious. "She's said she'd see you after Trig, behind the bleachers."

"Oh, very funny. I agree that all of this is a little ninth grade though." Orin sat down and shook his head, smiling. "I just don't want things to be awkward between me and Emmy next time she's assigned to protect me."

"If it's any consolation... she likes you, too."

"Nothing's changed though, Mox. It still can't happen."

Moxie sighed, a little frustrated. "Dude, JFK stepped out on Jackie the whole time. These things can be arranged. You know about the tunnels underneath, the unmarked cars... Come on. Live a little."

"You're my chief of staff, Mox."

"Not off duty. Off duty, I'm your friend first, and I can see how... solitary you're becoming."

"Screwing my Secret Service protection isn't going to cure that." He winced as he said it and Moxie saw it.

"Having a romantic relationship with a powerful woman would do you—and the Presidency—a world of good. Come on now. You both have everything to lose by being together. Doesn't that alone make you equals?"

"Emmy volunteered for a job which might mean taking a bullet for me. She's way, way above my level already."

Mox smiled fondly at him. "Big old romantic."

"Shut up."

"Well," she got up, "I'm turning in. Listen, Orin, think about it. That's all I'm saying. We can make it work."

When Moxie had gone, and Orin was alone, he sat with his head in his hands. The thought was so tempting, but really, he couldn't be distracted at the moment, even by something as pleasant as spending alone time with Emerson Sati.

Earlier, his closest advisors briefed him on the investigation into former President Ellis, and after what he learned, he knew he would have to make a decision on Ellis's pardon, and that his decision would not make his enemies happy. Brookes Ellis was up to his privileged ass in corruption—and worse, he was undoubtedly involved in human trafficking.

Orin shook his head. He would never understand the mind of someone whose ego was so out of control that he sought to control others to that hideous extent. Brookes Ellis had shown during his three-year presidency that he cared little for his public or the responsibilities of his office. Scandal after scandal broke in the press, but the President seemed to be made out of Teflon and merely dismissed the scandals as 'ephemera.'

Next, his chief of staff, Lester Dweck, had been taped by a journalist from The Washington Post during a drunken rant in a private club, talking about the 'girls' he could get for all his drinking buddies.

Dweck was an alcoholic, despondent about not getting the 'top job' himself, and despised, not only by those on the other side of the aisle, but by his own party leadership. He was lucky, or smart enough, to make sure he had 'collateral' on Brookes Ellis, who reluctantly appointed Dweck his chief of staff.

Ellis would keenly regret that decision. Dweck turned on his boss in exchange for a lesser sentence. Ellis denied all knowledge but by then it was too late. The Non-Stick President had finally gotten stuck.

So, Orin knew he could never pardon Ellis—hell, he didn't want to pardon him. The former administration filled him with disgust, and he wanted them all put away for a long time. He had directed his investigators to make sure the case was watertight before he would announce that a pardon would not be forthcoming.

So, as much as he would like to entertain the possibility of a relationship with anyone, let alone Emmy, Orin knew the country had to come first. He did hope that Moxie's good intentions wouldn't ruin the back-and-forth he and Emmy had—which alone would have to satisfy him.

He went to bed, and his subconscious tortured him some more with images of Emmy Sati naked and gasping as he made love to her.

A few miles away from Camp David, at a small-town high school, a group of men worked quietly in the basement directly under the school gymnasium. All around the school were posters for the next day's basketball game, a local championship against the school's greatest rivals.

The men worked silently and quickly, then as each one finished his particular task, the leader nodded, and they left the area. The leader went to check that the caretaker's body was well hidden, and then, just as quietly, they left the area. Tomorrow, the blast would be heard for miles, certainly at Camp David, and they would have handed President Bennett his first big crisis.

It was only the beginning of the horror they would unleash on the new president...

CHAPTER SEVEN

A loud knocking on her front door woke Emmy from sleep. She groaned and rolled over. "Just let me sleep in." She checked the clock. Ten a.m. Okay, so she had slept in. She got up and threw her robe on over the T-shirt and shorts she wore to bed and padded into the living room.

She wasn't prepared for what she saw when she opened the door. For a moment, her heart constricted, and all the breath left her body.

Zach beamed at her. "Hey, there. You must be Emmy."

Not Zach. Tim. She should have known he would come back. "Hi."

There was a long awkward pause, and Tim's smile faltered a little. "Is this a bad time? I can come back?"

Emmy blinked. "No, no... I'm sorry, please, come in."

She stood aside to let him in, her heart thudding heavily against her chest. Marge hadn't been exaggerating: Tom was Zach's double—almost. He was taller, lankier, but the mess of dark blonde hair, the bright blue eyes... yeah.

She pulled the robe tighter around her. "Tim?"

"That's me. Look, you seem a little startled, and I'm sorry for interrupting your morning, but is Zach here?"

"Tim... sorry to be rude but who are you?"

He grinned, a sweet smile that stretched across his whole face. "Sorry, I'm Tim Harte, Zach's cousin. From Melbourne?"

Emmy felt both a wave of sympathy and of fear. She took a deep breath in.

"Tim... I'm sorry to have to tell you that Zach died. A year ago."

She watched his reaction as the smile disappeared and shock took over. "What?"

Emmy, her innate warmth taking over, took Tim's arm and steered him into a chair. She sat opposite him. "He was shot and killed in the line of duty." This was so weird—how did Tim not know, already? The few members of Zach's family that had come to the funeral... surely one of them would have told him. "Tim? Did your family not tell you?"

Tim shook his head. "No... I don't talk to most of them. They can be... well, they're not the nicest people."

Amen to that, Emmy thought, then she remembered something. "Wait... are you the cousin who went to Australia?"

Tim nodded, his handsome face still pale. "I am. I didn't keep in touch with anyone, but Zach and I exchanged letters now and then, maybe once or twice a year, but it was my only link. Zach's the only decent one out of all of them. Was. Jesus." He put his head in his hands, and Emmy's heart went out to him.

"I'm so sorry, Tim. Look, I'll make us some coffee and we can talk."

She went into the kitchen, starting up a cup on the coffee maker, her mind whirling. Zach's cousin. Zach had told her about him, not in great detail, but enough to know that Tim was the one person in his family that Zach had a good opinion of. There really wasn't any doubt that he was who he said he was—the resemblance was uncanny—but her training kicked in. She'd have to make sure, but for now, she would take him at his word.

She took the coffee out to him, giving him a shy smile. "So, you didn't hear about Zach from the internet?"

"I'm not good with computers. Hell, my daughter says I'm a dinosaur when it comes to modern technology."

"You have kids?"

Tim smiled weakly. "Two adult rug-rats, both with Aussie accents. Me and their mom, Lindy, are divorced but things are pretty amicable, I'm glad to say."

Emmy smiled at him. He seemed such a sweet man. "So, you're pretty settled over there?"

"Very. I have a ranch outside Melbourne. Listen, Emmy. About Zach... I'm so sorry. I know how much he loved you and how much you must have loved him. You must have gone through hell."

Emmy nodded. This man had all of Zach's warmth and kindness, and she found herself relaxing in his company. "It was the worst day of my life when Zach died. I felt... broken."

"And now?"

She smiled a little sadly. "I'm getting there."

Tim sat forward. "Look, I know this must be a lot, and I hope me coming here hasn't reopened that wound." He studied her for a moment. "Do you have family here, Emmy?"

She shook her head. "Zach was my family. My neighbor, Marge, is a good friend, like a mom... I'm sorry, it seems strange to talk so easily to you, but you really are Zach's double."

Tim smiled and opened his mouth to speak when Emmy's pager went off. She looked apologetic as she grabbed her bag. "I'm sorry, that's work. I have to take it."

"Go ahead, of course."

Emmy read the page and felt the blood drain from her face. Tim noticed.

"Hey, are you okay?"

She shook her head and looked up at him. "No. Something's happened."

CHAPTER EIGHT

Emmy steered her car carefully through the throng of journalists, emergency service vehicles, and frantic parents. A plume of smoke rose from the high school in front of her. She saw Lucas Harper fielding questions from his men, and Emmy parked and went directly to him.

"Hey, Lucas."

"Em, thank God. Listen, the President heard about the bombing and wanted to come straight here. I told him we wouldn't allow it unless the place was secure, and we wouldn't impede the rescue effort."

Emmy nodded, seeing the faces of terrified students and parents. "How many?"

"Last count, thirty-two. That includes the caretaker who we think was murdered last night—obviously when they placed the bombs. C-4 on a timer. Luckily—if I can even use that word in these circumstances—the gymnasium was only just beginning to fill. Another ten minutes, and we'd be talking mass casualties." He sighed, shaking his head. "There's no way I'm letting the president come here at the moment. We'd just be taking the focus away from the emergency services."

"How's he doing?"

Lucas shook his head. "Not good. He's beside himself that this could happen, as you'd expect. Em, I need you at Camp David. We can't take this attack, so close to the president, as anything other than a warning."

"I agree."

"I'm sorry about your vacation."

Emmy smiled at him. "Lucas, really, don't worry about it. You want me protecting the pres?"

"Closely. I know he likes to chat to you; I think it would help if he had you there."

Emmy frowned a little. She was being used as a nursemaid? Lucas read her mind. "Em, you're an asset. That the President confides in you is an asset."

"Lucas, all he's confided in me so far is that he's thinking about getting a dog."

"It's a start."

Emmy drove to Camp David where she was met by Duke. He asked her what the scene of the bombing had been like. "Hell," she said simply. She couldn't stop thinking about the searing grief on the faces of those students and parents. In a heartbeat, their safe world was gone. It reminded her of the before and after moment when they told her Zach was dead.

Everything ends, just like that.

"Lucas tells me he wants me with the president."

Duke nodded. "He's up at Aspen with Moxie and Charlie Hope. The VP is at the White House."

They walked to the president's cabin and were let in by Greg, who quickly briefed them.

"They're talking about a live address from here to the nation. Moxie thinks he should go back to the White House."

"Maybe. If they're bombing near here, it's obviously a threat."

"Yup."

They went to main room and saw Orin Bennett deep in conversation with his advisors. He looked up and nodded at them, and Emmy could see the depths of sadness in his eyes. She nodded back, hitched up the side of her mouth in a reassuring smile, then smoothed her expression. It wasn't her place to make the president feel better; she was there to keep him safe.

Orin was preoccupied arguing with Moxie. "No, Mox, going back to the White House will make me look weak—as if I'm running away. We still don't know who was behind this, or if their motivation was to strike at us. It seems arrogant to leave when maybe I could do some good here."

Moxie and Charlie looked at each other, then Moxie sighed. "Fine. Vice President Hunt has told us she has a statement ready but won't release until after our message is out."

Kevin McKee spoke up then. "The statement is almost done and your speech for the address is in progress. In fact, sir, if you would excuse me..."

"Go, go. Thanks Kevin." Orin waved him away. He risked a glance at Emmy. He'd seen the small smile, appreciated it. What he wouldn't give to feel her arms around him now?

Focus. Kids were dead. Jesus, he couldn't imagine what those parents were going through right now. He finished up the meeting and instructed them to call in the cameras and lighting. "I'll do the address here, but I want it to be formal."

"You got it, Mr. President."

Moxie and Charlie stood. "Say, Agent Hill, would you mind escorting Moxie back to her cabin? We sent her agent off to help with the rescue."

"Of course, sir."

Moxie rolled her eyes but didn't say anything. She winked at Emmy as she left.

Alone with the president, Emmy didn't say anything, waiting for him to begin a conversation. He rubbed his eyes and sighed, smiling sadly at her. "You went to the site, I hear?"

"Yes, Mr. President."

"They won't let me go."

"May I be honest, Mr. President?"

Orin smiled. "Of course, Emmy, and please, while we're alone, call me Orin. Please come sit down."

Emmy hesitated, then nodded, moving to the couch. "Orin, your presence there at the moment would just create more problems. We would have to secure a perimeter which might mean parents not finding their kids or being denied access to the information they need. I know you wouldn't want that."

Orin sighed. "I wouldn't."

"Tomorrow is the appropriate day to visit and share your condolences, Mr—Orin."

He smiled at her, his green eyes soft. "Emmy, thank you for coming, for breaking in to your vacation. You don't know who much seeing your lovely face helps. I know that's inappropriate, but just for now, I had to say it."

Emmy didn't know what to say to that, her face burning with shyness—and pleasure. God, this man... she didn't know how it happened, but then his lips were against hers, and they were kissing. Sweet sensations flooded her body, taking her reason away, and his fingers were cradling her face. God, this kiss... wait. What the hell was she doing?

Emmy pulled away. "I'm so sorry, Mr. President."

"No, no, I'm sorry, that was... I'm sorry." His face was red, too, and he got up, chuckling. "I'm sorry but I'm not sorry, Em. I can't help myself."

Emmy stood. "I think perhaps I should be reassigned, Mr. President."

"Please, don't. I'm sorry, that was entirely inappropriate, and it won't happen again, I swear. God, what was I thinking?"

"Sir, it's okay, let's just forget it. You're under a great deal of strain, and it's an emotional day for all of us. Sir, honestly, it's forgotten." Emmy hoped he would believe her lie.

Orin studied her. "I swear, from now, I'll keep my feelings to myself."

Despite the situation, Emmy couldn't help feeling pleasure that he liked her. "Sir, I would appreciate that. I'd also appreciate that this stayed between us, but if you think you need to say anything to Lucas Harper…"

"I don't see any reason for that." He smiled at her. "Look, Emmy, if nothing else, I like talking to you. Can we be friends?"

"Of course, Mr. President."

They gazed at each other for a moment, the longing obvious, but also the realization they could never be together settling in. Orin held out his hand and Emmy shook it.

"Friends."

"Friends."

CHAPTER NINE

Orin Bennett hugged the woman whose daughter had died in the bombing. He refused to let the cameras in here, despite what Kevin wanted, needing this to be only about comforting the survivors and victim's families, not about boosting his own popularity. He was struck by the horror of what had happened as he toured the site. Bodies were still being found in the rubble of the gymnasium. The fatality count had risen to forty-four, and Orin met with each and every grieving family.

After leaving the school site, he went to the local hospital and met survivors, some with terrible injuries. Orin spent hours with them, always aware of how tired they were, or if they wanted to be alone, but empathizing with them. He allowed some reporters in at the end to take photos, with a proviso that the focus was on the victims and not him.

He was drained by the time they got back to Camp David. Meeting with his closest advisors and Lucas Harper, they discussed the claims of responsibility that had flooded in.

"As always, most of them we can dismiss straightaway as kooks. We always get at least ten claims from the same nut job groups who wouldn't be able to conjure an attack like this out of their asses. Excuse my language, Mr. President," Lucas added at the end.

Orin grinned. "Forgiven. So, now we come to the credible claims."

"The most likely group responsible is still the far-right splinter group led by Max Neal. Mr. President, as you know, we still think we could learn something from Martin Karlsson."

Lucas cleared his throat, glancing at Charlie Hope, who nodded. "Mr. President..."

"We need you to hold off on the announcement that you're not going to pardon former President Ellis," Charlie finished for Lucas. "If it gets out, then Karlsson will be too ticked to help us. He might side with his old roommate. Right now, he thinks there's still a chance his mentor Ellis will be vindicated. He might be open to talk, and anything—anything—we can get from him would help." He leaned forward, making sure his old friend was listening. "Mr. President, I assure you this bombing, however horrific, was only the beginning. Max Neal is a psychopath, a white supremacist, and a terrorist."

Orin shook his head in disgust. "What does he want?"

"Truthfully? Max Neal wants to bring you, wants to bring any President down who doesn't adhere to his Nazi-sympathizing world-view. The man is scum, Mr. President, and he won't stop until he's killed as many people as he can. Havoc. That's what Neal wants, sir, and he'll stop at nothing to get it."

Moxie stayed behind when the others left. He smiled at her. "It's been a long day, Mox."

"Awful, but this is the job, O. This is not the only one of these we'll have."

They sat in companionable silence for a few minutes, before Orin said quietly "Ellis is guilty as hell, Mox. There's no way I'm pardoning him."

"I know."

He studied her. "Do you think his crazies will do more stuff like this?"

Moxie met his gaze evenly. "I don't think there's any doubt. As soon as they know their precious Brookes is heading for federal jail, the floodgates will open. No one's safe."

Sitting in Lucas's debrief the next day, Emmy's mind kept drifting back to that kiss. God, if anyone ever found out... She dragged her attention back to what Lucas was saying.

"Obviously, because of the bombing, we've upped the president's protection as well as for key members of the administration. We're adding new members to the team as well as backups for you."

He sighed. "Listen, it's been a few rough days for everyone, but we can't afford to let our focus lapse even for a second. In a few days, President Bennett will announce that he will not be issuing a pardon for former President Ellis, and I think we all know the crazies will go, well... crazy, and the threats will flood in. The president has agreed to postpone that announcement until after we interview Martin Karlsson."

Duke raised his hand. "And how are we playing that? Is he under arrest?"

"No. He was asked politely to attend an interview to help out, and he graciously agreed. So, we're soft-balling, but I still want the important questions raised. Emmy, Duke, you'll lead."

"He won't be offended by mere agents interviewing him?"

Lucas shrugged. "I don't give a crap if he is."

There was a smattering of laughter. "Listen, folks, we knew at the beginning of this administration that we were in for a rough ride. I believe in you all. Thanks. That's all for now."

As they filed out, Lucas called Emmy back. "You got a second?"

Emmy nodded, but her stomach dropped. Shit. Had she and Orin been found out? But Lucas just smiled at her. "I've heard really good things about you. The President said you helped him with the situation out at NSF Thurmont. I always like to have one agent on my team who can act as a confidante to the people we protect, and it seems you're it this time. Good work. Em."

God. She felt horribly guilty as she thanked him and went back to the field office. Duke saw her face.

"Uh-oh. What's up?"

She hesitated, then nodded outside. "Can we walk?"

"We can walk. Let me explain evolution to you," he joked, and she laughed, shedding a little of her tension.

"Okay, pedant, may we walk?"

He followed her outside, grinning. "Feeling guilty because of the flirty-flirt with the pres?"

"Duke." Emmy shook her head. "Seriously, if anyone heard you... Anyway, it's weird when you ask me about my non-existent sex life."

"Em, you're my friend. I do not want to think about you having sex, let alone hear about it. No offense."

"None taken." Emmy studied him. "There's nothing going on."

"Hey, boo, you like him, right?"

"Yes, but I'm also committed to my job." She lowered her voice. "Duke... Zach gave his life protecting Kevin McKee. Do you honestly think he'd be happy if I threw everything I've worked for away? I cannot, I will not dishonor his memory like that."

"He'd want you to be happy, Em. Look, would it really be such a big deal? Jeez, you've heard all the rumors about presidents over the years. They've sneaked more women into this place than foreign heads of state."

"Yeah," she lowered her voice, "but they weren't protecting him, for Chrissakes."

"We'll deal with that if it comes to it." Duke shrugged nonchalantly, and strangely his casual attitude made her feel better.

"Can we talk about something else now?"

Duke gave her a smile. "Sure. So, when's Karlsson coming in?"

"Thursday. Let's go prep what we'll ask him."

If Orin and Emmy thought that only two people in the world knew about their kiss, they should have known better. An observer had looked through the window, seen the exchange, the blatant lust in

both their eyes. Orin Bennett and Emmy Sati wanted each other...
badly.

Whether or not the observer would keep the information to
themselves... it depended on how useful that information would be.

The observer smiled inwardly now, grabbed the burner phone
and went to call Max Neal.

CHAPTER TEN

"Beef or chicken?"

"Beef," both Emmy and Tim said at the same time and laughed. Tim touched his beer to Emmy's.

"Great minds."

The waitress smiled at them both and moved away from the table. They sat outside; it was an unseasonably warm day in DC, and Emmy smiled at her new friend. The restaurant, a Tex-Mex place, had been one of Emmy and Zach's favorites, but she hadn't been there for a year or two and was quite glad the entire staff was different, so no awkward questions were asked about Tim's resemblance to Zach.

And it was quite extraordinary. Emmy wondered if she should really be spending so much time with Tim because of it. After that first meeting, Emmy had called Tim to apologize for having to run out on him, but Tim had brushed her apology aside. "Hey, listen, I understand. But I'd like to see you again. Maybe talk some more?"

Emmy had readily agreed, and they'd spent time together on a couple of Emmy's off days. Tim was funny, erudite, and sweet, and although it was painful to be with someone who reminded her of Zach, of what could have been, Emmy also found his presence a balm —and a distraction from her turmoil over Orin Bennett.

"So," Tim said now, "how does one spend time in this city? I've done the McNuggets tour.

Emmy grinned. "The McNuggets?"

"You know, five minutes in the National Archive followed by Apollo ii and the Hope Diamond."

"Oh, dear God, man, you are a philistine," Emmy pretended to be disapproving. "I'm just going to have to educate you. Want a tour of the White House?"

"I thought they'd stopped that."

"They stopped the tours of the West Wing after 9/ii, but I can get you in. You'll have to be cleared by my boss, of course, so any dark secrets of yours, tell me now."

Tim pondered. "Well, I did tip cows in high school."

"Who didn't?"

He appraised her slight frame. "Can't see it."

"You doubt my cow tipping skills?" Emmy was enjoying teasing him; even after this short time, it felt like they had known each other forever. "Fool."

Tim grinned widely, swigging his beer, and as the server arrived with sizzling plates of fajitas, they both groaned with pleasure at the scent of the food.

"I usually don't eat fajitas in public," Emmy admitted, "because I always, always manage to spread the guac all over my face."

Tim immediately stuck his finger in his guacamole and wiped it on his nose. "There. Now you can spread away."

Emmy choked on her food she was laughing so much. "You loon. Listen, later on, Marge and I are going to see our dog at the shelter. Want to come?"

"Try to stop me," Tim looked excited. "I love dogs. And any excuse to spend more time with Marge."

Tim had been a huge hit with the older woman, who swapped up her Coca-Cola habit for a Sam Adams in Tim's company. Tim flirted up a storm with Marge, who cackled in delight every time Tim made a near-the-knuckle remark. Marge had nodded at Emmy one night after Tim had said goodnight. "Sweet boy, that."

Emmy rolled her eyes. "Boy? He's in his late thirties, Moo."

"Still. You could do a lot worse."

Her words had made Emmy feel a little uncomfortable, but now, sitting with Tim, she understood why Marge would say it. Tim was so easy to be with, no hidden agenda, no guile—although he was clearly a very intelligent man. He had told her that his desire to go to Australia had precluded his going to college, but that after a while as he grew older, he began to teach himself: reading endlessly, taking courses, just being inquisitive about the world.

"They say education is wasted on the young," he said now as they chatted about what he'd learned, "and it's true. There's so much to know, Emmy." He studied her. "You went to Harvard, I hear?"

Emmy nodded. "On a scholarship. I'd aced my bachelor's degree at college in New Orleans, but my tutor insisted on me pursuing my master's. She arranged the scholarship for me. I went to Harvard and was recruited from there."

"What did you study?"

"Criminal psychology."

Tim sat back, obviously impressed. "You're kick ass."

"Ha! Not really." Emmy had flushed red at the compliment. She glanced at her watch. "But what I am is late. I have to be at work by three."

"I'll drop you off at home."

As they drove back to Georgetown, Tim looked over at her. "Hey, tomorrow is Friday night—you working?"

"Unfortunately, so," Emmy sighed, but she didn't mean it. Working meant seeing Orin and... "How about Saturday night? Are you free? We could go see a movie or something?"

"Sounds good to me." He grinned at her with that smile that was so much like Zach's it made her heart thud with sadness. For a moment, she wondered whether they should invite Marge as a chaperone, but then she brushed the idea away. Tim knew they were just friends; her paranoia wasn't going to ruin that.

As she arrived at work, Duke was waiting for her. "Martin Karlsson will be here in an hour, and Lucas wants to see you."

Why did those words now strike fear into her heart? It was one kiss and no one saw it. Just chill out, woman.

She went to find Lucas. "Hey, Em, come on in."

Lucas seemed in a good mood. "We may have a lead on the bombers," he said, handing her a folder. "A local farmer noticed activity on his land near a barn he hadn't used for a few years. Nothing major, just that a light was switched on outside of it. He wouldn't have noticed, but he got up in the middle of the night to pee and saw it in the distance. Went out there in the morning and saw the doors had been jimmied. Inside: fertilizer."

"Which isn't unusual on a farm."

"No." Lucas smiled at her. "Until you factor in that the farmer didn't know where the hell it came from. He questioned his workers —as did we—but they're denying all knowledge of it."

"I don't understand. C4 was used at the high school, not fertilizer."

"I know. But we have to follow up and that farm is less a mile away from Camp David."

Emmy nodded. "Okay." She studied her mentor. "Not to rain on your parade, boss, but it doesn't seem like much of a lead."

Lucas sat down. "I know, but at this point, I'll take anything. If we can find out where the fertilizer came from and who bought it, we might have a chance. Max Neal's people have gone so deep underground, they're just ghosts. It doesn't make me sleep better at night. You have Martin Karlsson coming in?"

"Yes, sir."

"Well, any light he can shed is worth it. Get him on our side, Emmy."

"Yes, sir."

Emmy was surprised when she went to pick up Martin Karlsson from reception that he seemed to remember her. "Agent Sati, good to see you again."

"You, too, Mr. Karlsson. Would you come with me, please?"

"Of course."

They walked in silence through the field office, but it wasn't uncomfortable. Emmy offered him some coffee. "No thank you, but I'll take some ice water if you have some."

"Of course. Have a seat in here and I'll be right back."

"Thank you."

Emmy grabbed some ice water from the fridge and went to find Duke. "Karlsson's waiting."

Martin Karlsson actually smiled at them as they came in, even at Duke. "Ah, Agent Harte, hello again."

"Thanks for coming in to speak with us, Mr. Karlsson."

"It's Martin, and it's my pleasure. I know why you want to talk to me."

"Max Neal."

Karlsson nodded. "Agents, while I have many problems with this administration, I can assure you that if Max Neal had anything to do with the bombing at the high school, I will do everything in my power, give you ever piece of knowledge I have, to bring him down."

Emmy was impressed with the man. From her point of view, Karlsson was being genuine, but she knew first impressions were not always correct. Going by her gut was not an option here, although of course, it helped.

"Martin, perhaps you be would so kind to tell us how you met Max Neal."

"We met at Princeton. We were both members of an open society club although the organization's ethos ended up leaving Max unsatisfied and frustrated. He always complained that we didn't go 'far enough,' but what he meant by 'far enough' we could never get out of him. Max was a loner, didn't date, a good student, but he would spend his evenings writing political tracts and manifestos." Karlsson's mouth hitched up in a smile. "Of course, this was before the internet, so sadly, there's nothing online. He handwrote them all. God knows where they are now, but you could check his mom's attic."

Emmy grinned. "Well, that's a start at least. But seriously, sir, did he give any indication of being radicalized by any far-right groups around that time?"

"He certainly took notice of them, but to be fair to him, he never aligned himself with them. Not back then. Jump forward in time, it was when former President Ellis was in office that we started to hear about Max's group. Ostensibly, they were just a conservative group with minimal influence. Max would get in contact with me, and then if I agreed with him, I'd take his concerns to the president's advisors."

"Ever straight to the president?"

"No. As much as I admired President Ellis, I was never in his close circle of advisors. I couldn't be, you see, to do my job."

"Damage control."

Martin nodded. "Exactly. I had to be discrete from the chief of staff and his underlings."

"Lester Dweck." Duke said and shot a glance at Emmy. She nodded.

"What's your read on Dweck?" She asked Karlsson, whose eyes immediately flashed with anger.

"He's a king-sized asshole who wouldn't know the word loyalty if he was hit in the head with it." Martin stopped and sucked in a breath, looking away from their curious gaze. "Sorry, but that guy really pushes my buttons."

"So it seems," Duke said dryly, but Emmy was more sympathetic.

"Can I ask, Martin? What drives your loyalty to former President Ellis? No snark, I swear, I'm just curious."

Martin Karlsson nodded. "It's a legitimate question, Agent Sati. The Brookes Ellis I know would never, could never have done the things he was accused of. His politics could be, perhaps, a little too right wing at times, but human trafficking? I just don't believe it."

Emmy suddenly realized something about Karlsson. "Mr. Karlsson... are you a Democrat?"

Martin grinned. "Yes. I know, I know... a Dem doing damage control for a Republican president sounds contrary. But that's my job, regardless of party sensibility. Same with your job—you protect the president regardless of your own preference."

"We do."

"If we can get back to the questions," Duke said. "So, when did you lose touch with Max Neal?"

"A year ago, just after all this started. He just vanished. I didn't think anything of it until this week when you called. Now… it makes sense if he's a suspect in something. The one thing I can tell you for sure? He was enraged that President Ellis was impeached. Enraged."

CHAPTER ELEVEN

Later at the White House, Emmy reported back to Lucas on what Karlsson had said. Lucas nodded. "Yup, that ties in with what intelligence is saying. Neal's been sighted in DC over the week, so we're at Code Amber. Listen, I hate to ask, but Hank's out sick. Any chance you could pull double duty this weekend?"

"No problem," Emmy said easily, but she felt guilty about having to reschedule Tim. Not as guilty as I should feel, she told herself. "Listen, Lucas, I'm here now, so I'll stick around. I can catch up on paperwork and stuff until my shift starts."

Lucas smiled at her gratefully. "You're the best. Listen, I hear there's food left over from a brunch in the kitchen. Grab it before it goes."

As ever, at the promise of food, Emmy's mood lifted, and she went down to the kitchen. Since Inauguration, every time she was down here, she thought about that chat with the president.

Orin. He'd made her call him Orin, and now she struggled to think of him as the president when she wasn't on duty. The thought of him made her stomach warm and her belly flutter. She willed him to suddenly appear now, but the kitchen remained empty. She grabbed a sandwich and went back to the office to look through what intel they had received.

Emmy got so caught up in her work that she didn't notice the time fly by, and when she checked her watch, it was almost eleven thirty and her shift started at one a.m. She quickly went to the kitchen to wash up her plate and was just drying it when she heard his voice.

"Honestly, I'm beginning to think we should just call this our meeting place and have done with it."

She turned slowly to see the president smiling at her. She felt her cheeks flame. "We do always seem to be in here, Mr. President."

"Perhaps we're just foodies."

Emmy nodded, determined not to let the shine in his eyes make her giddy. "I can confirm that, sir. I was the competitive eating champion in my class at Harvard."

Orin laughed. "You were?"

"No, not really, but I could have given them a run for their money." Emmy felt more herself when she joked around with him; he was so easy to laugh with.

"I hear you're stuck with me for the whole weekend, Emerson. I do apologize." He didn't look sorry in the slightest, and she couldn't help grinning.

"It's a cross I shall have to bear, sir." God, she loved making him laugh that deep, throaty sound.

"I was just coming down for some ice cream," he told her. "Grab a bowl yourself."

"I'm good, sir, thank you."

"I thought we discussed that off duty, I was Orin?"

Emmy nodded at the clock. "It's only an hour until I'm officially at work."

"Which still means I'm Orin."

"Fine. I'm good, thank you, Orin. I'm more of a savory fan."

"Really? So, what's your go-to?"

"Well, don't tell the Surgeon General, but anything salty or meaty or umami-ey. That's not a word, I know. But really, a good flame-grilled steak or burger, or just a bag of really good potato chips. I'm drooling at the thought." She watched him eat his ice cream with obvious enjoyment. "Sweet tooth, Mr—Orin?"

Orin was scooping another large spoonful of ice cream into his bowl, and he grinned at her judgement. "I know. It's my vice."

"Just the one?"

His gaze met hers. "The only one I'm allowed at the moment."

A thrill shuddered down her body at the raw, naked lust in his eyes. "Yes, sir."

"Orin."

"Yes... Orin." She hadn't meant it to come out quite so meaningfully, but her voice had dipped to a low, husky sound.

Orin reached out and stroked a finger down her cheek, and she froze. His hand fell away. "I'm so sorry, Emmy. I don't mean to make you uncomfortable." He sighed, then gave a sad chuckle. "It's Murphy's Law that the day I get to be president, I also meet the most beautiful woman I've ever seen—and I can't do anything about it. Forgive me, this is inappropriate."

"Mr. President... for the record," Emmy felt her face burn, "I feel the same way. But my job is to protect you, and I cannot let anything interfere with that." She held his gaze. "I lose concentration for one moment—the wrong moment—and... I could lose you. The country would lose a great man."

Orin smiled and looked around the room. "Emmy... is anything likely to happen right now?"

"No, sir."

He held out his hand. "Dance with me. Do you know how many times I wanted to ask you to dance at that Inauguration Ball, Emmy? You in that red dress... my God. Every man in the room wanted you. Especially this man."

Emmy knew she should say no. Her training screamed at her to stop this, but she couldn't. She took his hand, and he drew her into his arms. There was no music, but they moved around the room as if there was. His hand was on the small of her back, and she could feel how hard and athletic his body was as he pulled her close. Her senses were reeling, but she dared not look up into his eyes...

"Emmy," he whispered, and the sound of her name being spoken with so much tenderness brought back memories of Zach. The thought stopped her dead. She pulled away from him and tried to smile.

"I'm sorry, Mr. President. I can't." She took in a shaky breath. "Sir, if you prefer that I be transferred away from your detail..."

"No," he said, and gave her a smile, shaking his head. "I'm sorry, that was inappropriate and entirely my fault. Please, finish your meal, Agent Sati. I'll leave you alone. Goodnight."

"Goodnight, Mr. President."

And he was gone. Emmy sat back down, trembling. Has that actually just happened? It was so unprofessional on her part—and his—but she understood the attraction because she felt it, too. Jesus, Sati, what were you thinking? If she'd stayed in his arms a moment longer, she knew without a doubt that they would have been kissing—and then what? Screwing in the Lincoln bedroom?

God, the one man in this world she wanted was the one she couldn't have—ever.

Darn it. She was going to have to ask Lucas to transfer her away, no matter what Orin said. This couldn't happen again. If she lost focus for one second, Max Neal's men might get to Orin, and the thought of him ending up like Zach—Christ, the pain ripped through her like nothing else since the day they told her Zach was dead.

Surely, she didn't feel the same about Orin Bennett as she had about her beloved Zach? Unbidden, the answer came back to her.

Yes.

Oh fuck. She had fallen in love with him.

"Don't be fucking ridiculous," she muttered to herself, irritated and confused. "A few fun times in his company? That's not love, that's a crush."

She went to find Lucas. Her boss, who looked exhausted, was about to leave to go home, and Emmy's courage failed her. "Just wanted to say, if you want a second eye on the intel, I'm all over it. I'd like to be part of the investigation properly, not just on the periphery."

Lucas patted her back. "Don't stretch yourself too thin, Em. You're protecting the Leader of the Free World. That's enough for anyone."

Shit...

CHAPTER TWELVE

Orin had returned to the Oval, his emotions in turmoil. He had to do something to distract him from how he felt about Emmy Sati. He asked Peyton Hunt, his serene VP, to come see him. His old college friend took one look at him and asked what was wrong.

"I think I need to date," he said, somewhat awkwardly. "To feed the press's greed, and for my own peace of mind. I just don't know how."

Peyton smiled at him. She had always played the big sister role to Orin, being a few years older, and right up until his election, Orin had always assumed their roles would be reversed, that Peyton was on track to be America's first female president. It was only when Peyton came to him, recently widowed, and she told him she wouldn't be running, that he'd realized she had never wanted the top job.

"But you, Orin, you must run."

He'd told her he would—on condition that she be his vice president. Eventually, she agreed.

Now, she sat with her old friend and nodded. "I think it would be good for you, and yes, maybe it would ease the press' fervor. I know you want to concentrate on the issues that are important, but I think that in order to represent the country the way they expect, you should have someone by your side." She studied him. "Anyone in mind?"

Yes, yes, yes, the gorgeous Secret Service Agent less than a few yards away. "I was going to ask if you knew anyone... suitable. God," he rolled his eyes. "What are we defining as suitable?"

"Well," Peyton sat back and crossed her legs. "Someone who matches your intelligence, your compassion. Someone who makes you laugh and challenges you. For aesthetic reasons, a human rights lawyer or a lobbyist from a foundation. A charity maven."

Orin sighed. "You know anyone?"

"Actually, I do. I've been thinking of someone in particular for a while now, but I hesitated. Mostly because she's not long out of a relationship, but also because of the first one hundred days. But if you feel you're ready?"

Orin was silent for a moment. He wanted to tell his old friend that he was falling for Emmy Sati, but he didn't want to risk Emmy's career. He trusted Peyton, but this was bigger than friendship. No, this was right. He would take himself out of the situation. "So, who is she?"

"Nahla Delaney. She's a human rights lawyer from England working here in Washington for Kushner, Flint and Harrison. Word is, she'll make partner before the end of the year. Fierce in court, erudite, intellectual... and a lot of fun. Beautiful, too—just FYI."

Peyton took out her phone and flicked to her photos. She handed the phone to Orin. Nahla Delaney was indeed beautiful: long dark hair, dark hazel eyes, and a charming smile.

"She's a little younger than you, early thirties, but I think you two would hit it off."

Orin handed her back the phone. "Can you set up a date?"

"I'll ask her certainly."

Orin smiled his thanks. "How does this work?"

"Well, you obviously can't go out to dinner, so we arrange a dinner here. In the private residence, we'll get in a guest chef from a four-star restaurant to cook for you."

Orin looked vaguely alarmed. "Jeez... for a first date?"

Peyton relented. "Well, maybe not. But still, we don't want Nahla being asked what she ate, and she tells them a pickle and a bag of potato chips."

Orin laughed, a little uncomfortably. Potato chips. Emmy would be delighted if she were served that. God, stop it. You cannot have Emmy Sati. Get over it.

"Well, I'll leave the details to you. What do I do? Send flowers? An invitation?"

"We'll take care of all of that."

"It all seems a little clinical."

Peyton shrugged. "It's the way it is in the major leagues, Orin."

After Peyton had left, Orin went to the Lincoln Bedroom to read, but his mind was still on the way Emmy felt in his arms. As he fell asleep, he began to dream that she knocked on his door, right now, in the quiet of the early hours. He would watch from the bed as she slipped out of her clothes and moved towards him.

He held out his arms, and she went into them and finally her skin was against his, her breasts against his bare chest. Her arms curled around his neck, and her lips, her soft sweet lips, were against his as his own arms held her tightly. She was so tiny, so small against his big frame that he knew it was his turn to protect her as they began to make love. The moment his cock slid into her wet warmth, he knew it was right, hearing her moan, gasp his name as he thrust ever deeper into her.

Then she was gone, even before he could reach his peak, like a mist. The dream was over.

Emmy Sati was once again way, way out of reach.

"So," Tim said the following Monday evening when Emmy finally managed to rearrange their movie night, "You sure you won't have to work tonight?"

She grinned at him. Instead of going out, they'd decided to stay at home—her home—and watch a movie on her flat screen. Emmy had cooked a simple but delicious pasta dish, and now they kicked back with some beers and a vast bowl of popcorn in front of them.

Tim grinned at her, and in the evening light, it was easy to pretend it was Zach. No fair to Tim, Emmy told herself. Tim nodded at the screen. "You've seen this before?"

"Many times. It was one of Zach's favorites, that's why I chose it." She sighed. "Tim, I want to say again how sorry I am that you came all of this way, and Zach... he would have loved to reconnect with you, I know it."

Tim clinked his beer bottle against hers. "Amen to that, Em. But I still got to spend time with you, and that's no small thing." He hesitated. "I can easily see why he fell in love with you."

Emmy swallowed a lump in her throat. "That's a sweet thing to say." She met his gaze and he smiled

"All of it true."

He reached out to stroke her cheek, but his hand fell away before he made contact, and he looked away, embarrassed. "Sorry. I forget myself."

Emmy felt like crying. "Don't be. Let's be honest here, Tim... there is something there. But I don't know if it's because you resemble Zach so much—and that isn't fair to you. You deserve better." She hesitated. "And there's... someone. Someone I can never be with, but just now, I need to get over him."

Tim smiled sadly at her. "Who couldn't you have?"

"You'd be surprised. Look, it would be so easy to fall into a relationship with you, Tim, but it wouldn't be good for either of us. Besides, your heart lies in Oz." She grinned at him as he took her hand and squeezed it.

"You're right, kiddo, I know. A guy can dream, though."

She smiled at him. "Ha, you wouldn't like me. If Zach were here, he'd tell you about my incessant eating, the snoring, the cookie crumbs in the bed."

"Shocking." Tim was chuckling.

"You've seen what I do to fajitas."

Tim pretended to shudder. "Scarred for life. It was a like a were-wolf with a fresh lamb."

"I know, right? And you haven't seen me eat steak. That's not pretty."

"I bet you don't even have it grilled—just brought to the table, still mooing."

Emmy grinned widely. "See, you know me too well already."

"Plus, the gas. Man, you can fart, woman."

Emmy cackled with laughter. "Dude, if I had farted in front of you, you would have known it."

"All that meat."

"Like an Aussie rancher doesn't know all about gas."

"Like sonic booms."

"Gross!" But they both doubled up laughing. When they had caught their breath, Emmy smiled at him.

"Buddies?"

Tim gave her a fist bump. "Besties, always. Now, let's watch this movie. I see Alicia Vikander is in this, so at least, when I go home alone tonight, I'll—"

"Do not finish that sentence," Emmy giggled at his mischievous face. "T.M.I."

"Fair enough."

"Give me some popcorn."

"Bossy."

"Shut up."

CHAPTER THIRTEEN

Nahla Delaney was as beautiful, intelligent, and witty as Peyton had painted her. She had agreed—eventually—to have dinner with the president, and now as they sat alone in his private dining room, Orin found himself enjoying her company.

Peyton had indeed arranged a guest chef to come in and cook for them, and they had enjoyed sea bass with asparagus, beautifully prepared, with a sauce vierge, followed by roast lamb, tender and juicy. Now, they were eating a green tea sorbet with a delicious and delicate lime mousse.

So far, the conversation had revolved around Nahla's work as a human rights lawyer, and their talk had naturally turned to the Brookes Ellis sex trafficking case.

"I know you can't tell me specifics, Mr. President, but if I can be any help? The whole thing is disgusting, but all too prevalent, I know."

Orin nodded. "The whole thing is repellent, but to have the leader of this country so entrenched in such dealings... it's hard to process."

"I can imagine." Nahla put her spoon down. "Does rather put one off one's food, but I have to say, that was delicious, Mr. President."

"Orin, please, and thank you. I'll pass your compliments to the chef."

"Please do." Nahla studied him. "Orin... why am I here? I mean, I'd never turn down an invitation from the White House, but this seems... are we on a date?"

Orin hadn't expected her to be so forthright and for a moment, he was stuck for words. "More of a... hello."

"A reconnaissance mission?" She was teasing him now, and Orin grinned, relaxing.

"I'm out of practice at this," he said, with a wry smile, "and now things are more complicated."

"Sure," Nahla said, chuckling softly, "I'm sure I was vetted to the nth degree. Let me guess. I'm educated, in a respectable job, and reasonably attractive."

"Very attractive," Orin amended chivalrously, "but yes, you do tick all the boxes. I hate to admit it."

"Hmm." Nahla nodded slowly, then smiled at him. "Except, both you and I know that despite the fact we're friendly... there's no chemistry."

Orin laughed then. "Man, you really are brutally honest."

"Orin, you're a bachelor president, an Independent. You've already instigated a huge change to how the Presidency is perceived, and thank God for it. So, don't sell yourself short when it comes to choosing your partner in life, for goodness sake. Don't let the American public bully you into a marriage of convenience. Tell them screw it, you're going to marry for love and no other reason."

Orin smiled. "Believe me, I want to. But it's a matter of..." He trailed off. Could he ask this woman about the ramifications of beginning an affair with a subordinate? As the president? "Hypothetical?"

Nahla smiled. "Go for it."

"What if the person I was interested in... worked for me?"

Nahla sighed. "Well, then you'd get into workplace law and fraternizing. It could be seen as coercion if the person was a much lower rank. What are we talking here?"

"Ha," he said, shaking his head. "I can't say."

"But there's someone?"

He nodded. "There is. Look, Nahla, I'm sorry to bring you into this charade, but I'm not sorry to have met you."

"Same here, Orin, really. And besides," she gave him a wicked smile, "if we slept together, I couldn't honestly make a play for attorney general in a few years."

Orin raised his glass. "I can see it. And speaking of White House Roles... you know Flynt Mitchum is retiring in October? We'll begin short-listing soon. I'd add your name to it without hesitation."

"As a thank you for not sleeping with you, sir?"

Orin laughed and sighed. "Nahla, I swear, what a shame about that damn chemistry."

"I know."

They went to have drinks in his private lounge, and at midnight, they shook hands, parting as friends and probably future colleagues. Nahla sized him up and down. "You're a gorgeous man, Mr. President. Whoever she is, I'm sure you can make it work."

Later, Orin went to find Peyton, whom he knew would still be at her desk, to tell her about the date. But when he found her, he saw that her face was tear-stained. "What is it, Pey?"

She shook her head, trying to smile. "Nothing. Just one of those nights when I miss Joe so much it hurts so damn bad."

Orin hugged his old friend. "I'm sorry."

Peyton wiped her face. "I don't even know what set me off, except... I was reading a letter from one of the parents of the kids who died in Maryland." She looked at him. "Don't waste time on not loving who you're meant to, Orin." She rubbed her face. "Talking of which—"

"—Nahla is beautiful, funny as hell, smart... and there was absolutely no chemistry between us."

Peyton sighed. "At least you tried." She studied him then got up and closed the door. "Orin, there's been talk."

"Talk?"

"That... you're sweet on your personal detail. Agent Sati. I can't begin to tell you how damaging it could be, how unsafe it could make you, to get involved with her."

"No," Orin said, his heart sinking. "No, you don't need to tell me that."

"Also, that young woman has been through enough. Do you know how hard she had to work to get here?"

"I do, Peyton."

She watched his face. "Orin?"

Orin stood and paced for a moment. "What if I told you that I'm in love with her, Pey? That I can't stop thinking about her."

"The press would destroy her, and so the reputations of any female agents in her wake. This is bigger than the two of you."

"Didn't you just tell me not to waste love?" Orin realized his voice was rising and held up his hands.

Peyton waited for him to calm himself. "Come on, Orin, you know all of this. Stop behaving like a lovesick teenager. If Nahla didn't work out, we'll find someone else."

"No." Orin stood. "I'd rather just... concentrate on the job."

"Good."

Peyton was right. He needed to grow up and stop mooning around. He had a freaking job to do. Orin went to bed that night, berating himself for once again losing focus. He knew what he had to do. First thing in the morning, he would call Lucas Harper and arrange for his entire protection to be rotated out for new agents. Not singling Emmy out was the least he could do.

CHAPTER FOURTEEN

"It's no biggie," Lucas said, a few days later. "The president just wants to make sure that we're rotating through, making sure we all get the same experience. Duke, Em, you'll now be on the vice president's detail until further notice. Hank and Chuck, you move over to Kevin McKee..." He went on reassigning agents to various White House staff, but Emmy stopped listening. Orin was creating distance. Good. That was good. Yeah, it hurt, but in one way, Emmy was relieved. It would make things easier on both of them if they didn't have to work so closely.

Of course, not being on his protection also meant... no. Don't even think about it. Nothing has changed. He's still the president, and you're still just you.

"Sir?" She raised her hand and Lucas nodded.

"Go ahead, Em."

"Any news on Max Neal?"

"Still nothing. Listen, I know you talked to Karlsson already, but I'm suggesting... Em, ask him out for drinks, loosen his tongue. Find anything, because at this point, I'll take anything. The local FBI field office in Maryland is ready to give up on the investigation, and that's not good news for anyone."

Emmy nodded and went back to her desk to call Karlsson. She didn't think she would get anything more from him, but it was worth a shot. She found it frustrating that Lucas wouldn't let her get more in depth with the whole thing, but this was at least something.

Martin Karlsson agreed readily—a little too readily, surprising Emmy, but also giving her hope he might have something new to tell her.

Martin Karlsson was waiting at the coffee house when she met him two days later. He stood to greet her and caught her off guard by kissing her cheek. "Agent Sati."

"Mr. Karlsson, thank you for coming."

"It's Martin, please. Can I get you a drink?"

They sat at a table in the window and made pleasant small talk for a while then Martin smiled at her. "I have to say, I was absurdly pleased when you called, Emmy—I can call you Emmy?"

"Of course. I just wanted to check in with you after the conversation we had the other day at the field office."

"Nothing more to report, I'm afraid." He studied her. "You look disappointed."

"I admit I am. We seem to have hit a brick wall as far as the investigation into Max Neal. When you were at college, I believe Max Neal was funded by his parents?"

Martin nodded. "He was, but I know that ended as soon as Max became more right wing. When they died, they left him nothing."

"Which makes me wonder now how he can afford to go so deep underground. That's my thought—he must have funding to be able to disappear entirely. No paper trail, no credit card, paying everything in cash. And to have the inside knowledge we presume he does..." She trailed off, thinking. "Princeton."

Martin looked confused. "Yes?"

"Martin, did either of you know Kevin McKee at Princeton?"

Martin shook his head. "No, he's a few years younger than the both of us. His older brother Clark was ahead of us and head of the chapter of our fraternity."

"Which was?"

"Phi Kappa Alpha. But I know Kevin McKee didn't join a fraternity when he was at college."

Emmy considered. "Secret societies?"

"Possibly, and certainly Max would have loved that kind of thing. But, once again, I don't know for sure. Secret societies always gave me the creeps." He smiled suddenly, and Emmy noticed that it lit up his otherwise blandly handsome features. "Possibly because I was never asked to join one," he admitted with a chuckle, then his eyes met hers.

"Emmy... I understand if you want to say no to this, but I'd like to see you again. Out of work. I find myself quite... enchanted."

Emmy felt her face burn. "That's very kind, but..."

She was saved by Martin's cellphone buzzing and he smiled ruefully. "Sorry, I have to get this."

"Of course."

She watched his expression change from relaxed to shocked to anger and wondered what the hell was going on. Martin hung up the phone and looked at her with narrowed, unfriendly eyes, all his warmth gone. "Did you know about this?" He was already standing, gathering his coat. Emmy was confused.

"Know what?"

"Your boss," Martin almost spat, "has decided to act as judge, jury, and executioner. He's not pardoning Brookes Ellis."

Emmy wasn't shocked. "Martin, surely you saw this coming?"

"No, I didn't fucking see it coming! Brookes Ellis is an innocent man, Agent, and I—" He stopped, pinching the bridge of his nose, trying to calm himself. "I'm sorry, I know it's not your fault. I have to go."

And he left her standing, mind whirling at what had just happened. Emmy sat down, sipped her still warm coffee and checked her phone. The news had indeed leaked that Orin wasn't going to pardon Brookes Ellis. "There is overwhelming evidence," he was quoted as saying, "that Brookes Ellis was one of the instigators and operators of a known sex trafficking ring. He funded the import of young men and women for purposes of supplying sexual gratification. Federal charges will be brought against him and his co-conspirators, and I fully expect that former President Ellis will be found guilty on all charges."

Emmy raised her eyebrows. Orin wasn't holding back, but she was surprised Lucas hadn't told her the announcement was coming today, especially when he knew she was meeting Karlsson.

She drove home, wondering if she ought to call Lucas and ask if she should come into work. The apartment building was quiet as she climbed the stairs to her floor. She knocked at Marge's door but there was no answer. Odd. Marge rarely went out—but then again, she might have been picked up by her daughter, Eva, who had come into town. Emmy shrugged and went into her own flat.

In a second, everything changed. Her hackles went up just moments before she was grabbed from behind and thrown across the room. Emmy scrambled to her feet as her attacker came for her, his fist smashing hard into her jaw. Emmy staggered back, her head hitting the door jamb hard, knocking her dizzy, and she slumped to the floor. Her attacker kicked her hard in the stomach and she groaned. She fumbled for her sidearm as the attack continued, and she rolled tightly into a ball to protect herself. She heard the click of a safety and her adrenaline spiked. She rolled over, whipping out her gun and shooting at her attacker as he fired back. Emmy felt the sting of a bullet in her side, but knew it was just a flesh wound. She managed to get off another shot, hitting her assailant in the wrist of his gun-carrying hand, and he cursed loudly, kicking out and catching her forehead with the heel of his boot.

Emmy's head snapped back, and she felt pain screech through her body. Her attacker kicked the gun from her hand and dropped to his knees, his one good hand fixing around her throat, and squeezing. Emmy choked and the vision in her eyes began to blur.

"Get off her, motherfucker!"

Almost unconscious now, Emmy heard Tim's voice, full of shock and rage, just as the darkness came for her and she gave into it.

CHAPTER FIFTEEN

Orin was yelling. Orin didn't yell… ever. But today was different. In the Oval with Kevin, Issa, Moxie, and Peyton, Orin was incandescent with rage. "How the hell did this leak? I had specific instructions that the embargo on the Ellis pardon was midnight."

"Sir…" Issa looked pale and shaken. As press secretary, it was her job to make sure nothing got out that the president didn't want to, and she'd failed him. How, she didn't know. She hadn't briefed the press or begun a strategic leak which sometimes was necessary when sensitive information was about to be in the public domain. The pardon, or refusal of it, had been on lockdown, and now Issa looked upset and close to tears.

"Sir, I swear, I have no idea how this could have leaked. We even kept it held close from our staff."

Orin sighed and rubbed his face, trying to calm himself. "Look… who knew?"

"You, me, everyone in this room. Lucas Harper. Charlie Hope." Peyton looked as angry as Orin felt. "Your personal protection. Not that I think it could be them."

"But we can't discount them," Kevin added smoothly. "Who was in the room when you made the decision last week?"

Orin thought back and his heart sank. "Agent Sati."

There was a knock at the door. "Come in."

Jessica appeared, her face grim. "I'm sorry to interrupt, Mr. President, but Lucas Harper is here and insisting on seeing you."

"Have him come in, Jess. Thanks."

Lucas Harper looked green and sick. "Sir, forgive my intrusion but something has happened." His voice shook, and he was trembling with shock. Orin had never seen him so worked up.

"Lucas, come sit before you fall down." He nodded at the others, dismissing them all except Moxie, who went to grab some water for Lucas.

"What is it, Lucas?"

"Sir, Martin Karlsson is dead. He was found murdered outside his home thirty minutes ago."

"Jesus." Orin hissed. "Are we sure it was murder?"

Lucas nodded. "He was shot in the back of the head, sir. One bullet, point blank. There's something else you should know. Before that, he had met Agent Sati for coffee."

Orin's heart failed him. "What?"

Lucas nodded. "An attempt was also made on Agent Sati's life at her home."

Orin stared at him in horror. "Is she okay?"

For a moment, time stopped, and Orin felt his heart bang uncomfortably against his ribs before Lucas nodded.

"Is she okay?" He repeated, trying not to let the desperation creep into his voice.

Lucas nodded. "She was beaten and kicked pretty badly, and she suffered a flesh wound from a bullet, but otherwise she's okay. It's my understanding that she managed to disarm her attacker before being knocked unconscious. A relative then appeared to help her. Her attacker is in custody."

"I want to talk to him."

Both Moxie and Lucas shook their heads. "No, sir, I'm sorry, this is a federal matter and if you interfere..."

Orin sighed. "Where is Emmy now?"

"She was treated at George Washington but discharged herself."

"I want her protected," Orin said, trying to keep his voice from shaking. "And I want to see her."

Moxie and Lucas exchanged a glance that Orin couldn't read. "What?"

"Sir, this is all part of Agent Sati's job."

"I don't care. Someone tried to kill her, and I do not take that lightly. She's part of this family." He chewed his lip. "I'd like her to be taken to Camp David for the next few days to recover. We're making the trip up there ourselves tomorrow night."

"I'll put it to Agent Sati, sir, but as you can appreciate, it is her decision."

Orin nodded, holding back from making it an order. He desperately wanted to see Emmy now, to hold her in his arms, and it was almost killing him not to just blurt out how he felt. Instead, he thanked Lucas.

Moxie stayed behind after Lucas had left. "Careful, Orin. Your feelings for Emmy are starting to show."

"Right now, this moment, I don't care," he said, shortly. "Jesus, Mox… she's hurt, and it's my fault. What do you want to bet that this had something to do with the announcement today?"

"We can't know that."

"Why else would someone want to attack her?"

Moxie sighed. "Okay. But look, we don't know anything much about her personal life. Maybe it was some old boyfriend—"

"On the same day Karlsson is killed?" Orin looked skeptical. "The same day they had coffee together?" Ouch. What if Emmy were dating Karlsson? Not the thing to dwell on right now, you idiot.

Moxie stared at her friend. "Fine. But bringing her to Camp David?"

Orin shook his head. "I want to see her, and this seemed the best way."

Moxie got up and went to her friend. "Look. I know how you feel about Emmy Sati, and I know you tried to put a cap on those feelings. Maybe it's time we tried a different approach."

"Like what?"

"If you're both at Camp David, and you both want the same thing... there are ways."

Orin knew he should shut this down immediately, not even consider it. But his mouth opened and out came the words. "Make it happen, Mox."

Emmy listened calmly as Lucas told her she was being moved to Camp David, but inside she was a whirlwind of emotions. Fear, excitement, trepidation... the thought of seeing Orin was appealing, but, she told herself, it was just because of the possible concussion. Her body ached, her head hurt, but otherwise she felt fine.

Tim, on the other hand, was a little put out. He sat beside her as the doctor gave her a last check-up. "So, you're being forced to go to Camp David now?"

"Not forced no, but if my boss wants me there..."

"You just got beat up, Em. Surely they can consider that?"

"I think, in a weird way, they're doing it for my own protection."

Tim's shoulders relaxed. "Oh. In that case..."

Emmy held his hand. "Tim... you saved my life. I'll never forget that."

"It was the least I could do, kiddo, and you'd already done the hard graft by the time I got there. Dude was down and out."

"Tim, he was choking me. You stopped him." Emmy touched her bruised and sore throat unconsciously. That had been the most terrifying part of her whole ordeal, and all she had been able to think about was never seeing Orin Bennett again. "Listen, while I'm at Camp David and you're still in Washington, would you do me a favor and look in on Marge once in a while?"

"Sure thing, sweetheart." Tim kissed her forehead, then looked around as Duke and Lucas returned. "Guys, take care of my... sister," he finished with a smile at her, and Emmy knew instantly he was right. They had grown so close, almost like siblings and now, with a pleasant thrill, she knew. She had family.

Tim said goodbye, and Emmy promised to call him soon. "You'd better, cutie."

Duke grinned at Emmy. "Hey, slugger."

"Hey, loser."

Even Lucas smiled at their banter. "So, Duke's your taxi service for Camp David. Your home has been secured now, so you can go pack a bag, grab whatever you need to."

Emmy nodded. "Thanks, Lucas. Listen, I can work. I'm fine. So, while I'm at Camp David…"

"While you're there, you can do light duties," Lucas gave her his best gimlet eye, "And I mean light. No protective detail or physical stuff. At least a week."

"But I can help with the investigation?" She looked so hopeful that both Duke and Lucas had to laugh.

"Yes, Agent Scully, you can help with it." Lucas smiled at her, his eyes questioning. "Are you sure you don't want to transfer to the FBI?"

Both Duke and Emmy made derisive sounds, echoing the rivalry between the agencies and Lucas tried to look disapproving and failed. "Okay, well, the car's outside when you're ready. The president wants to see you as soon as you get there if you're up to it."

"Of course, sir."

Emmy excused herself to use the bathroom in her room and stared unhappily at herself in the mirror. A dark bruise was forming on her forehead, and there were scratches and cuts on her face. On her jaw, another bruise was already turning black. "Jesus you look like a horror story," she muttered to herself, then dipped her head to splash water on her face.

In the car, Duke looked over at her. "Hey, you okay? Don't mind telling you, there were a lot of scared people worried about you."

"I'm okay. I'm sorry about Martin Karlsson. Underneath his rabid support for Brookes Ellis, he was a nice guy."

Duke nodded. "Yeah, I think you're right."

"Which makes me wonder why anyone would want him dead."

"What did you two talk about?"

"Just Max Neal and his time at Princeton. We know there's a leak in the White House now, and I think... I think I might have a lead."

Duke's eyebrows shot up. "Who?"

Emmy hesitated. "Kevin McKee." She waited for his reaction.

Duke's shoulders slumped. "Em... you can't be the one to... God, Em, if anyone found out that you were digging into McKee, they wouldn't see an agent. They'd see a bereaved woman trying to find a reason to punish McKee for her lover's death."

"I know, I know, which is why I'm telling you and not Lucas. Help me, Duke. I may be way, way off the mark, but there's a scholastic link between McKee and Neal, and I want to see if there's more to it."

Duke chewed this over. "Okay, but you know it's a longshot, right?"

"I do, but right now, we haven't got a lot to go on."

Duke nodded, and they drove in companionable silence for a while before he spoke again. "Em... can we talk about the elephant in the room?"

"What's that?"

"That dude, Tim..."

"Yeah. Zach's cousin."

"You two having a thing?"

Emmy didn't mind Duke asking; it must have been so strange for him to be suddenly confronted with a man who so resembled his dead friend. "Definitely not. Tim's become like a brother to me. I won't deny that early on, there might have been a little mutual crush, but no. Just friends. And he saved my life, so there's that."

"Amen, sister. He seems like a really good guy."

"He is."

They smiled at each other. "Good genes."

"Yeah, I think he and Zach got the lion's share of the good ones."

"Word."

Emmy sighed as they drove. "Duke... do you think it's a little weird that the president ordered an agent to Camp David for R&R?"

Duke smirked, and she grinned at him. "What?"

"An agent, yes. You? No. Come on now, Emmy. I know he's fond of you. Those late night chats?"

"Nothing has ever happened." Not quite a lie...

"I know that. I know you. But Em, let's be real. The pres likes you a lot. You know he had someone to dinner the other day, a date?"

Ouch. Jealousy shot through her, but Emmy pushed it away. "No, I didn't."

"Word is that even though the woman was great, the pres wasn't feeling it, because he's already smitten with someone else."

"Jesus, Duke, if Lucas ever, ever heard anything..."

"Lucas is an adult," Duke said shortly, "and these things happen. Anyway, I've said enough."

When they reached Camp David, Duke accompanied her to the Aspen Lodge, then with a wink, left her with Moxie Chatelaine to wait for Orin Bennett. Moxie hugged her. "God, you scared us, girl."

"Sorry, Mox." Emmy took a deep breath in. "Listen... why?"

Moxie smiled. "I think you know the answer to that, Emmy. Now, look, I told Orin I wanted to talk to you before he came in. He sulked about it," she chuckled, and Emmy laughed, "but he agreed because this is... unprecedented. Also, if he's reading the situation wrong, I don't want to put you into an uncomfortable position, so to speak."

"He's not." Emmy's voice was quiet, but steady. "He's not reading the situation wrong."

Moxie patted her hand. "Then... I can ask him to come in?"

"Yes."

Moxie smiled. "Then we'll make it work, Em. Don't worry about anything. Don't worry about Lucas or your job. Just...especially this week...just be. There will be no questions from anybody."

Emmy swallowed hard. "Okay." Her composure broke then. "What am I doing?"

"The most natural thing in the world, Emmy. You can't help who you love."

Emmy nodded. "I know."

"That's why he wanted to come here. Here, the world can go away. Here... it's a different world. You can be together."

Emmy felt her eyes widen, not really believing what she was hearing—or what she might be about to do. "How?"

And then she heard his voice behind her, and as she shot to her feet, Orin Bennett smiled at her.

"Because there are some perks to being president, my lovely Emmy."

CHAPTER SIXTEEN

Moxie smiled at them both and then quietly left the lodge.

Orin gazed at her. "God, your poor face."

"I'm okay." Emmy's voice was scratchy, her heart beating way too fast, but then Orin moved swiftly across the room and took her firmly in his arms. His mouth met hers, and Emmy's senses reeled as they kissed.

"God, Emmy, if anything had happened, if he'd killed you..." Orin groaned, his fingers sliding into her hair. Emmy sank into the embrace, her defenses completely down as her lips moved against his.

"I'm okay, I'm okay," she murmured against his lips.

When they finally broke apart, gasping for breath, Orin's arms tightened around her.

"I'm crazy about you, Emmy Sati. God help me, I don't want to risk your career or mine, but I can't stop thinking about you."

Emmy struggled with her own feelings, then her shoulders slumped. "I feel the same way, and that's not something I can reconcile. I want you, Orin, I do, but you're my boss."

Orin stroked the back of his fingers down Emmy's cheek. "This is madness, I know."

"If something happened to you while I was supposed to be protecting you..."

His lips were against hers again, and this time she didn't pull away. The kiss went on and on and Orin drew her in closer and tighter. She could feel his erection, hot and long against her belly and it thrilled her. If he fucked her here, right now, she wouldn't stop him. Hell, every fiber of her being wanted him to do just that.

"Emmy..." They finally broke away, needing oxygen, and Orin leaned his forehead against hers. "Emmy, Mox told me..."

"There are ways. That's what she said. There are ways." She felt as if she were jumping off a cliff, but right now, Emmy didn't care.

Orin nodded. "There are. Are you sure, Emmy?"

Fuck it. "Yes."

He kissed her again, smiling. "We'll work it out. I swear I won't let us interfere with your job. Or mine."

"Orin, just promise me something. Only when I'm off duty. When I'm on duty, it's professional all the way. I cannot live with the thought that you'd get hurt because I was distracted by how I feel about you. That's not me. I'm good at my job."

"You're great at your job, Emmy, although I can't fathom letting you take a bullet for me."

"That right there is why I'm hesitant. That's my job, Orin. If it happens, you will let me do just that. That's a deal breaker."

He sighed but nodded. "I'll just have to make sure no one takes a shot at me." He smiled at her and she relaxed.

"You will."

They sat in silence for a moment, Orin's fingers tangled in hers. "I hate to say this, but I do have a meeting now." He sighed. "Emmy, have late drinks with me tonight, here at Aspen—and stay. Nothing needs to happen if you don't want it to."

Their eyes met and held. "I do. I do want it to."

Orin's smile was soft, loving. "Me, too."

Emmy leaned against him, and he kissed her tender forehead. "How on earth is this going to work?"

"Plausible deniability, Emmy."

She smiled up at him, and he brushed his lips against hers again. God, it felt so right to be close to him. "I should go."

"Of course. Later, then."

"Later."

Back in her own cabin, Emmy came back down to earth. What the hell had just happened? Had she just agreed to be the President's mistress? His fuck buddy? What was she thinking?

Duke came to find her later, and they went to dinner, although Emmy had no appetite. Emmy saw the president sitting at the top table talking to Mox. She looked away quickly, not wanting her face to turn red, or to give anything away. Still, when she was walking back to her cabin, and she and Duke were alone, she had a shock.

"So," Duke said, his voice lower than normal, "the plan is this. You come to my cabin at nine p.m. Mox and the pres will go out for their normal late-night walk and talk. Pres will be wearing the same clothes as me and we swap. Pres comes to meet you."

Emmy stopped, shocked to her core. "You know?"

Duke grinned. "Of course I know. Moxie and I have been plotting." He studied Emmy's reaction. "Don't worry, babe, it's all handled."

Emmy blinked, shaking her head. "I always knew you were a pimp."

Duke laughed loudly, attracting some attention, and he steered her away from the others. "Girl, damn it, just enjoy. You're two people who are attracted to each other. Forget the job for one night. Scratch that itch."

All night Emmy was waiting for someone to come tell her that it was all a prank, but she still went to Duke's cabin at nine. Duke grinned at her. "Condoms in the night stand," he said, making her blush.

Alone, she waited for Orin to arrive. Was she really doing this? She told herself it wasn't relevant that she'd showered and shaved her legs just an hour ago. Thoughts of Zach flew into her brain, and she nearly changed her mind. She knew he would have never begrudged her happiness, but would he think she was being reckless?

There was a soft knock on the door and, taking a deep breath in, she opened the door. Orin stepped into the cabin, smiling at her. "Hey, there."

"Hey." Her voice was gravelly, and to distract herself from her nerves, she locked the door. Orin took her hand and led her into the living room, drawing her down with him as he sat on the couch. "Don't be scared, Emmy. Nothing has to happen that you don't want."

She gazed at him, then leaned in. As soon as her lips touched hers, all doubts and concerns flew away. They kissed, softly at first, then as Orin's fingers tangled in her hair, his tongue caressing hers, Emmy straddled him on the couch. "Touch me, please" she whispered, and he smiled, sliding his arms around her waist.

Emmy slid her hand down to his groin, cupping his long, thick cock through his pants, hearing him moan with arousal. No turning back now.

"I'm going to take you to bed now, beautiful Emmy."

She nodded, and he stood and lifted her with ease, carrying her to the bedroom. Setting her down, he began to unbutton her dress as she pulled his shirt out of his pants. Their gazes met, and they both chuckled. "Can you believe this is happening?"

She shook her head. "No, but I'm going to go with it."

Orin laughed and peeled her dress from her, sucking in a breath at the sight of her body. "Jesus, Emmy, you're stunning..."

She silenced him with her mouth as she pushed his shirt open, then kissed his hard pecs as he fumbled with the clasp of her bra. She grinned as he cussed quietly, then Emmy reached around to unhook it. "Men and bras. You can rule the world, but give you a pretty standard bra clasp..."

Orin laughed then swept her down onto the bed, covering her body with his. He ran a hand slowly over her belly. "I've been fantasizing about you since the first day we met."

Emmy gave him a mock-disapproving look. "Mr. President, you have a country to run."

Orin grinned. "And as your president, I must tell you, that I intend to conquer your South..."

As he made his way down her body, Emmy giggled. "That was such a bad joke, so, so... oh!"

His mouth was on her sex, his fingers having already tugged her panties down her legs, and as his tongue lashed around her clit, Emmy began to tremble, giving up the last of her control.

Orin Bennett, she decided, was a spectacular lover. He made her come, his tongue flicking her clit until she was crying out his name, her limbs liquid, her mind whirling.

As she panted, he moved to take her nipples into his mouth, each in turn, nibbling and sucking at them until they were almost unbearably sensitive. Emmy had his cock in her hands, stroking and massaging it against her belly until it was diamond-hard and trembling.

She helped him roll a condom down his large cock, and he hitched her legs around his waist. He looked down at her with gentle eyes. "One last time... are you sure?"

Emmy nodded, and with one long thrust, Orin was inside her, both of them sighing with the release of the tension between them. They moved together, Emmy tightening her thighs around his waist as his cock buried itself deeper and deeper inside her. They kissed as they made love, breathless and smiling. Their bodies fit together so perfectly that Emmy could hardly believe this was their first time.

She felt so small and precious next to his big body, and it was a feeling she didn't know well. Weirdly, she felt safe with him, even though it was her job to protect him, and she told him that. Orin smiled down at her. "Good. I want you to feel safe. It kills me that your job is to protect me, but I'm selfish. I want you around."

Neither of them felt like talking any longer as they drove each other on to an explosive, all-consuming orgasm. Emmy let herself go, losing herself in this man, clawing at his back, kissing him passionately. Orin dominated her body as she neared climax, and when he snaked his hand down to massage her clit, he sent her over the edge and her back arched up, her head rolled back, and she gasped as she came, her body vibrating with the sweetest sensation.

"God, Orin... Orin..."

He buried his face in her neck, his lips against her throat as he came, groaning her name quietly but with such intensity it thrilled her. As they recovered, he cradled her in his arms, his eyes shining. "You made this old man very happy, Emmy."

She chuckled. "Not so old."

He stroked her hair back from her face. "Thank you for trusting me, Em. I'm aware, in my position, this could be seen as an abuse of power. If you ever, ever feel like that..."

"I won't. I have my own agency, Orin." She sighed. "I meant what I said. When I'm on duty, this never happened."

"Understood. And look, only Mox and your friend Duke know. We'll keep it that way. For now."

Emmy smiled, a little relieved. Orin kissed her and went to the bathroom to deal with the used condom.

I just fucked the President of the United States. She stared up at the ceiling of the cabin. She knew she should be—what? Ashamed? She was anything but. It had seemed so right. Looking at it logically, both she and Orin were single people—no. Emmy knew what she had done was reckless, stupid, and could endanger her job, but she couldn't regret one moment with this man.

She sensed his scrutiny. He was leaning on the door jamb of the bathroom, looking at her. "God, you're beautiful," he said, his voice tender. "Just look at you."

He came back to bed and lay down beside her, sweeping his hand down her body. "Every inch of you." He trailed his lips along her jaw, then kissed the hollow at the base of her throat, before propping his head up on his elbow. "We can make this work, Emmy."

She didn't really know what he meant when he said 'this' but for now, she would just assume sleeping together, although who knew how it would work when they were back at the White House.

But then her attention was taken by Orin making love to her again, and Emmy knew that whatever happened, her life had changed forever.

CHAPTER SEVENTEEN

Orin nodded and grunted his way through his morning briefing, hoping that it didn't contain anything too serious. Afterwards Moxie chuckled as they walked back to Aspen. "Did you hear any of that?"

"Give me a break, Mox, I'm exhausted." But he grinned. "It's not easy being the Leader of the Free World."

Moxie cackled delightedly. "Especially when you've been, um, up all night."

"Mox."

"Oh, come on! Give me some detail! I did run interference for you."

Orin chuckled. "You did." He rubbed his eyes. "If you thought if I scratched that itch, I'd get over it, you were wrong. I'm crazy about her, Mox."

"I know, doofus. Why do you think I set this up?" Moxie was smiling, then her smile faded. "But it's going to be a lot harder at the White House. We might need to bring in some more allies."

Orin shook his head. "No. I promised Emmy. No one else knows. If Lucas Harper found out..."

Mox frowned. "Orin... nothing comes without sacrifice. If this thing with Emmy is more than a hook-up, then decisions will have to be made. She knows she won't be able to protect you and you? I know you—you would rather die than let someone you care about take a bullet for you."

"God." Orin sat down heavily. "It's her career, Mox. How can I ask her to give it up? How monumentally selfish would that be?"

"Well, you can't. But this thing can't be more than sex. Don't fall in love with her."

"Mox, you realize you encouraged this? Now you're telling me to hold back? What if I want more?"

"Then Emmy will lose her job, possibly even be prosecuted for sleeping with her protectee."

Orin groaned. "Shit, Mox..."

"You needed to get laid, and you liked her. Emmy likes you, too. You're adults. But if it gets serious..."

"I got it."

Moxie get up and patted his shoulder. "Dude, I'm not saying you can't be happy, but you both have to be realistic. If you and Emmy want more, one or both of you is going to have to give up your job. I'm not trying to rain on your parade; it's just I've never seen that look in your eyes before."

Orin raised his eyebrows. "What look?"

Moxie smiled at him, her eyes soft. "Love, Orin. Love."

Emmy was feeling equally uncomfortable as Lucas came to see how she was. As she sat with her colleague, her thighs still aching from the marathon sex session with their boss, she felt guilty, embarrassed, and utterly unprofessional.

But not regretful. Last night had been the most erotic, sensational night of her life, and she knew that she was hooked. Even now she recalled the way his mouth felt closing over her nipple, or his long, warm fingers stroking her clit until it became rock-hard and her vagina flooded with desire.

His long, thick, magnificent cock sliding in and out of her... Emmy bit her lip to try to drag her attention back to Lucas.

Her boss had a sheaf of papers in his hand. "The entire White

House staff's personal files. Everyone up to and including the President. You wanted in. Well, this is it. Find any link, however tenuous."

"Actually, I already have one."

Lucas sighed. "I know. Em... Kevin McKee has been profiled up and down. It was he who persuaded President Bennett to run. It was McKee who was credited for a large part of getting him to the Oval."

"This isn't some left brain hiccup, Lucas. He went to Princeton, just like Max Neal and Martin Karlsson."

Lucas sighed, holding up his hands. "Fine. Just, look. You find anything, come to me. We can't risk any whiff of a witch-hunt because of Zach. I know that's not the case," he added hurriedly, seeing the grim look on Emmy's face, "but it is a complication."

"Fine."

When Lucas had gone, Emmy made herself some tea and sat down with the files, trying to focus on her work. Every minute though, she kept reliving the touch of Orin's fingers on her skin, his gentle caresses, his masterful way of fucking her... damn. Emmy closed her eyes and let out a long shaky breath. She hadn't had any sleep, but she had never felt more alive, more awake.

She grabbed Orin's file, unable to contain herself, but it didn't tell her anything she didn't already know. In fact, she thought to herself rather smugly, I know more about him than this file will ever know.

She grinned to herself as she imagined adding to the file.

Orin Bennett's military and political prowess is matched by the enormous size of his cock, and his excellent and energetic lovemaking. He is also above average in charm and sexiness and can make a woman come by just looking at her.

Emmy snorted to herself. She could imagine how agency heads would love to know all that. She put down Orin's file and took up Kevin McKee's.

She hadn't had a lot to do with the man, never having been assigned to him because of his connection to Zach's death. Before that, he'd hardly registered on her radar. To Emmy, he was just another vanilla pretty boy who used his looks and charm to get what he wanted and was pretty harmless. She read through his college transcripts. Graduated magna cum laude with a degree in political science, the valedictorian in his year, after which he went on to attend Harvard Law.

First job was junior partner at Dewy, Random and Lesser in New York before making full partner less than a year later. Family was old money from New Hampshire. Emmy rolled her eyes. "Pretty boy with all the gifts."

McKee sought out Orin Bennett after Orin's successful congressional run and offered to manage his presidential run, wanting only the communications job in return.

Emmy sighed. Nothing out of the ordinary. She grabbed her laptop and typed in 'secret societies at Princeton.' She knew that actually secret societies were banned, a law going back to Woodrow Wilson, but that didn't mean they didn't exist. She read about the aboveground societies but couldn't find any evidence that McKee, Karlsson, or Neal were ever members. She'd have to look deeper than a Google search.

Her personal cell buzzed, and she glanced at it, then smiled. Having trouble concentrating while State people brief me on nuclear proliferation. If the world ends, it's your fault. O.

Emmy giggled. Well, if the three-minute warning comes, I have an idea how we could spend that time...

She laughed loudly when the reply came back. Twice.

She loved that Orin was completely without ego; he really was the most unusual president.

Which gave her an idea. Maybe she was looking at this all wrong. She should be trying to link members of the current organization to the last administration. She pulled up a file with all of Brookes Ellis's staff and tried to cross match them with any members of Orin's closest circle. Not that easy, she thought, half an hour later. Someone was dirty; she knew it, and God help her, her gut was telling her it was McKee.

At lunchtime, she went to the dining hall. A quick glance around told her that Orin wasn't here yet, and anyway, she could hardly go sit with him. She grabbed a plate and went to help herself from the buffet.

"Hey, Agent Sati."

The man himself. Emmy plastered a smile on her face as she turned to see Kevin McKee in line behind her. "Mr. McKee."

"Come on, Emmy, we're off duty. It's Kevin. How're you feeling? Those bruises look nasty."

"They're fine, really. I'm okay."

"I hear you kicked the attacker's butt."

"I had help." Emmy didn't like the way he was looking at her—but maybe she was just feeling guilty about suspecting him. His smile was friendly enough, and there was even some admiration in his eyes.

"Don't knock yourself down. Hey, come sit with me and tell me about it. The news that an Agent was attacked was leaked, sad to say, and the press are already making their own minds up at this point."

"They're linking my attack to Karlsson's murder?"

"They are."

Emmy sighed. They found a table and sat down to eat. Maybe this was an opportunity to find out about Kevin's background. But as they began to eat, Emmy suddenly lost her appetite when Kevin started to speak.

"Listen, I've been wanting to talk to you for a while. About Zach. God, Emmy, I can't tell you how sorry I am. He was such a good guy—the best."

Her mouth dry, Emmy put down her fork and nodded. "Thank you. He was."

"I keep thinking of that day, the day he died. The gunman came from nowhere and at first, we didn't know Zach had been hit."

Emmy's hands were trembling. She'd never asked, nor been told, about the particulars of that day. It was enough to try to process that Zach was gone forever. Now, though, she didn't want to stop Kevin. She needed to hear it to gain some more closure and move on. "What happened, exactly?" She said, her voice breaking slightly.

Kevin sighed. "We were at Foggy Bottom, a meeting at the Watergate. Nothing huge. I believe it was about a speech we were coordinating with an environmental group for the campaign. We were just in the parking lot near that old British telephone box they've got there. The first shot zinged past my head, I remember, and then Zach was yelling and pushing me into the car. I got in and turned back, then..." He hesitated.

"Please go on, no matter what."

"There just seemed to be blood everywhere, like it was raining. Zach... he dropped. He'd taken a bullet straight to the chest. My driver screamed off, and I couldn't see what was happening after that. I'm so sorry, Emmy."

Even after all these months, it hurt like hell. Emmy closed her eyes, willing the tears to stay back. Her Zach, her best friend, her love. Gone, ended, stopped—just like that. Suddenly the loss of Zach along with the residue of shock from her attack began to weigh down on her, and Emmy excused herself.

She went back to her cabin and curled up on the bed, finally letting the tears come. She didn't notice the passing of time until she felt two strong arms slide around her, and she was drawn close to Orin's chest.

"Kevin told me what you talked about, and he was worried he'd upset you." Orin murmured against her temple. Emmy closed her eyes and let herself be held. Right now, he wasn't the president—he was a man who had come to comfort his lover. She tilted her face up to his and felt his lips against hers, gentle and loving.

They kissed until they were breathless then Emmy reached down and pulled her T-shirt up over her head. Orin's eyes searched hers. "You're sure?"

She nodded. "I need you, Orin, please."

Orin kissed her again, unbuttoning his own shirt, and then they were stripping each other quickly. Orin lifted her legs over his shoulders. "I want to taste you, pretty girl."

He buried his face in her sex, and Emmy moaned as his tongue lashed around her clit, teasing it, making it rock hard and uber-sensitive. "Orin, I want to taste you, too."

Orin turned his body so she could take his cock into her mouth as he continued to pleasure her. Emmy slid her tongue down the silky shaft, feeling how hard the muscle underneath it was, how it quivered as she caressed and sucked on him. She loved his salty skin, the way his cock shuddered when her tongue teased the sensitive tip.

With one hand, Orin was teasing her nipples, each in turn, until they were rock hard; with the other, he slid two fingers in and out of her sopping wet cunt until she was bucking against him, coming hard as his cock pumped thick creamy cum onto her tongue.

Emmy swallowed his seed as Orin righted himself and kissed her, his hands pinning hers to the bed. "Christ, Emerson Sati, I've never wanted anyone as much as I want you..."

Emmy rolled a condom down his cock, quickly, urgently, needing him to be inside her, and when Orin thrust into her, hard, she cried out in ecstasy.

Their gazes met and held as they made love, Orin slamming his hips against hers, Emmy tilting upwards to take him in deeper. His lips were rough against hers, his hands clasped almost painfully on hers.

Emmy came again, explosively, her back arching up as the sweet release overwhelmed her. "Oh, God, Orin... Orin, don't ever stop..."

Orin groaned, burying his face in her neck as he too reached his peak, then they collapsed together, panting for air.

For a brief moment, Emmy felt as if she were in someone else's body, but as Orin excused himself to use the bathroom and then came back, she smiled up at him and held out her arms. He went into them, kissing and smoothing the damp strands of her hair that were stuck to her forehead away from her face. "Have I told you how Goddamn beautiful you are?"

She grinned. "Not too shoddy yourself, Mr. President."

Orin chuckled. "Emmy... you should know. I'm in this. You and I. Us. We need to make this work; we have to do whatever it takes." His lips brushed along her jawline. "I tried to put you out of my mind, knowing it would be almost impossible, but it didn't work."

"I heard you had a hot date at the White House." She grinned at him to make sure he knew she was fine with it.

Orin nodded. "And she was a delightful woman. But she wasn't you."

Emmy flushed with pleasure. "I have to warn you... I'm far from perfect."

"Who is perfect? And how dull would that be?" He drew her close, and Emmy rested her head on his chest. God, he smelled good, like soap and clean laundry. She ran her hand over his flat stomach, feeling it quiver under her touch.

"How are we going to do this? I mean, here at Camp David, it seems pretty easy, but when we're back at the White House, it's going to be more difficult."

"We'll make it work. You'd be surprised what we can do." Orin grinned at her and then sighed happily as her hand snaked down to stroke his cock. "Emmy... you realize I'm insanely crazy about you, right?"

Emmy grinned at him, then straddled him, moving the tip of his cock against her wet sex. "Right back at you, Commander."

His cock was straining to be inside her then, and she guided him back inside, riding him slowly at first then as their passion ignited, harder and faster until they were both crying out, and laughing.

CHAPTER EIGHTEEN

Just before six p.m., Orin got dressed, leaving her in bed alone. He gave her a regretful look as she lay, just covered with a sheet. "I hate to leave you, Emmy."

She flashed her breasts at him which made him laugh.

"Tease." He sat on the bed, leaning down to kiss her. "I could always cancel my six o'clock meeting."

Emmy shook her head. "No way, buster. You have a country to run."

Orin grinned, and his hand slid under the bed to stroke her clit. Emmy tried to look disapproving but gave in as his fingers worked on her. She shivered through a mellow orgasm then smiled up at him. "One hell of a parting gift."

Orin smiled. "Later?"

"Later."

Alone, Emmy showered, smiling to herself as she soaped her skin. Her sex still felt sensitive as if one touch from him would make her come again. Emmy dried herself and threw on some sweats. She would go for a run through the woods here before it got too dark, getting rid of the some of the excess energy the lovemaking had left her with.

She passed some other agents and staff on the running paths, nodding to them and smiling, but with her earbuds in, she didn't stop to talk. She pounded the path, deep into the woods. She was surprised she wasn't feeling more battered from the attack which was still only a couple of days ago, but apart from the bruises, she felt fine.

Better than fine. Orin Bennett had complete dominion over her body, and Emmy loved that. She felt like a sexual being again, desired and desiring, wanted and wanton.

Which meant... she had a decision to make. Not yet, she told herself. Not here. She would just enjoy the few days left here at Camp David, then they would figure out the rest of it.

Deep in thought, she didn't notice that evening had fallen, and she was still running away from the camp. She turned, stopping to catch her breath, pulling her ear buds out to listen to the dusk. She panted hard until her breathing returned to normal. Her skin felt tingly—and not in a good way.

Emmy scanned around her. There was no one else out here—no one who wanted to be seen anyway—but she couldn't help feeling she was being watched. She narrowed her eyes, scanning the trees.

Paranoia.

Emmy began to run back towards the camp, and halfway back, she imagined she could hear someone running behind her. Closer... closer... she turned...

Nothing. No one. "Fuck's sake," she breathed to herself. "Get a grip."

She ran back to her cabin and let herself in. Again, that feeling of being watched crept over her. She put her hands over her eyes and shook her head. "No. Stop it."

Still, she checked the entire cabin. The files she had been studying were neatly on her desk. Shit. Maybe she should have returned them to Lucas before now. She gathered them up and went to his cabin.

Lucas looked surprised to see her. "Hey, you've been running? I thought the point of you being here was to rest?"

"Exercise is good for relaxation," she grinned at her boss. "Here. I didn't find anything useful in these."

"I didn't think you would, but at least it may have allayed some of your fears. Especially about Kevin."

"Hmm." Emmy remained noncommittal. "Listen, I talked to the president, just in passing." She could feel her face burn at the lie. "Seems he wants me to stay here for the duration of his visit. Something about being extra-vigilant about safety."

"Well, I'm not surprised. He was insistent on you being protected, at least until we find out if Karlsson's murder is linked to the attack on you."

Emmy sighed. "Is it wrong I actually feel bad for Karlsson?"

"Not at all. Despite his strange adoration of Brookes Ellis, he seemed like an okay guy."

"He was, actually." Emmy smiled. "And he was a Democrat, did we tell you that?"

Lucas looked bemused. "Really?"

"Really. He told me."

"Huh."

"What?"

Lucas shook his head. "No, it's just... never mind."

Emmy decided not to push it. "Anyway, as I said, nothing in these files. They didn't seem particularly in depth."

"Nope, they're not, but that's the best we have at the moment."

"So, these files aren't everything about everyone?"

"No. Sorry if I gave that impression. These are practically what we hand out to the press. For some reason, the agency is being cagey about releasing the personnel files."

Emmy let it go. At least she didn't have to worry that she'd left the files in her cabin. Man, her head was all over the place now. Maybe she should quit, try something else. It would certainly make her life easier...

"Em? You still with me?"

She blinked and smiled at her boss. "Yeah, sorry."

Lucas studied her. "You still look tired."

That would be the marathon sex sessions. "I'm okay."

"Sure there's no concussion? I think the doctor should check you out."

"Honestly, Lucas, I'm fine." Emmy started to walk toward the door. "But I'll get some rest, don't worry."

Making her way back to her cabin, Emmy was so lost in her thoughts she didn't notice Kevin McKee appear beside her, and she jumped a little when he began to speak.

"Emmy, I wanted to say I'm sorry again. I know I upset you earlier."

Emmy stopped. "Kevin, it's fine, it's okay. I needed to hear it. I've been burying my head in the sand about Zach." She started to walk again, hoping he would leave her alone but instead Kevin kept up with her.

"I feel bad. Look," he touched her arm, "Can we talk? In private?"

Emmy's hackles went up immediately. "I told you, Kevin, there's no need."

Kevin laughed a little self-consciously. "It's not about that, it's... man, I used to be good at this."

Emmy realized in horror he was asking her out. Nope. Shut this down. "Kevin, if you're talking about what I think you are, I think you should know... I'm seeing someone."

Your boss.

Kevin gave a good-natured shrug. "Ah well, can't blame a guy for trying. 'Night, Emmy."

Emmy watched him walk away. That was weird. They'd barely said two words to each other before now... he knows. He knows you suspect something.

Emmy shivered suddenly. Men like Kevin were insidious—did he really think he could distract her by appealing to her ego? Asshole.

Instead of going back to her cabin, she went to find Duke. He was playing pool in the bar with Hank and Greg but tapped out when she asked him if she could talk to him.

Outside she pulled him aside. "You up for some off the books snooping?"

"Always. Who's our mark?"

Emmy fixed him with a look and saw his face fall. "Oh, Em, really?"

"Yes, really." She was a little irked now. Why was everyone so preoccupied with defending Kevin McKee?

Duke sighed. "Fine. But this is two favors you owe me. What do you suggest?"

"Just a little close scrutiny. Know what he is doing when he is doing it. Who's on his detail? Can we get assigned? And by we, I mean you, because he just asked me out, and it would be awkward."

"More awkward than screwing the big man?" Duke kissed back at her. He had a point.

"Look, I'm just saying... I'm going to go to Princeton and get a read on his time there, and I need you to make sure he stays in Washington while I do."

"You know you could get into a lot of trouble for this?"

"More trouble than screwing the big man?" She grinned as she shot his own words back at him and he gave her a begrudging smile.

"Fine, I'll talk to Lucas."

"Yo, boss, you wanted to see me?"

Moxie was still chowing down on her sandwich as she sat down with Orin in his cabin. He dismissed his secretary and waited until they were alone before he spoke. Orin drew in a deep breath. "Mox... I need you to put a poll in the field."

"Sure thing. About?"

He studied her for a moment. "About the American public's reaction to the president's lover being a member of his security detail."

Moxie nearly choked on her food, then laughed. "Oh, ha. You got me."

"I'm serious, Mox."

Moxie put down her plate and swallowed her food. "You're serious?"

"Yup." He sat down opposite her. "Look, I'm not dumb, I know we can't frame the question that way—"

"—ya think?" Moxie interrupted, incredulous. "Orin, this could torpedo your whole presidency, you realize that?"

"I do. But here's the thing. I've found the person I want to spend the rest of my life with."

Moxie stared at him. "After sleeping with her once?"

"Twice," he said a little smugly, but then his face was serious again. "Mox, I knew it before Emmy and I had sex. Come on now. You never heard of love at first sight?"

"That's for teenagers and hokey romcoms. Orin, you're the President of the United States!" She got up and paced around, and Orin waited for to calm down. Eventually, she sat down. "We have to make it a governor, and it can't be his security detail. It has to be some other subordinate. Neither one is married."

His heart lifting, Orin smiled. "See? How hard was that?"

"That isn't hard. It's the fact that when and if you two go public... damn it, Orin. Her job will be forfeit. Have you talked about this with her?"

"Not in so many words. I wanted to get your read."

"My read is that you are insane. Jesus, can't you two just have this thing in private?"

Orin sat up straight. "I want a future with Emerson Sati, Mox."

"You're in love with her?"

He nodded, not wanting to say the words aloud until he'd said them to Emmy.

Mox gazed at him unhappily. "Even if Emmy doesn't lose her job, can you really see the First Lady also being responsible for taking a bullet for her husband?"

"Don't be stupid, Mox."

"I'm not the one being stupid. Can you not see the shit show this is going to bring down on all of us?"

"Because two people fell in love, Mox?"

"This is so much more than that, and you know it. The press will paint Emmy as a gold digger or a whore." Moxie sighed. "Look, at least give it six months. If you still feel the same—"

"I won't change my mind, Mox. Put the poll in the field."

At ten o'clock, Duke came to swap places with him, and Orin went to Emmy. Her smile when she saw him was worth all the grief that Moxie had given him. He kissed Emmy hello.

"Hey, come sit with me."

He stroked her face gently, wishing he could kiss the bruises on her face away. "In a couple of days, we have to go back to the White House."

"I know," Emmy sighed, "and the bubble bursts."

Orin shook his head. "No. Listen, I want to lay all my cards on the table here and now, Emmy. I love you. I think I've been in love with you from the moment I met you. I want to be with you, and I don't want to hide it."

Emmy's eyes filled with tears. "You love me?"

"I do," Orin smiled at her, "Very much. I think we get each other. With you, I don't feel the weight of my job or anything else. And, God, I want to make you happy, Emmy Sati and purge that sadness from your lovely eyes. Not that anyone can replace Zach."

Emmy smiled at him, moved beyond words. "Orin Bennett," she cupped his face in her palm, "I love you, too. You've helped heal me in so many ways. For a long time, I thought it was impossible, the two of us. Now I know to not be together is the impossible thing."

Orin's smile grew wide across his face. "That's what I think, too. But, it's also important to me that your career should not be forfeit."

"That's kind, but not realistic."

She leaned into him, and he breathed in the scent of her hair and her skin, felt the warmth of her body heat. He couldn't imagine a life without her now, but she was right. Maybe Mox had been right, too. Give it six months.

So, they talked late into the night, planning their secret love affair as best they could, before making love again. When Emmy was asleep, Orin slipped from the cabin and went to wake Mox. "You're right," he said. "For Emmy's sake. We need to wait."

Moxie, half-asleep, gave him a relieved smile. "Thank God."

Emmy slept deeply and didn't waken even when the intruder opened the door to the bedroom, and it gave a loud creak. He stood silently over the sleeping woman, the white sheet tucked around her naked body. God, she really was beautiful. He watched her slumbering for a few moments, wondering what she would do if he woke her, kissed her, made love to her.

Of course, now he knew. Orin Bennett was screwing this little beauty, and from what he had overheard earlier, the president was serious about her.

What a shame Emmy Sati was poking her nose into things she shouldn't. It meant that all their plans would have to be moved up. Yes, a shame. She had already lost one great love and soon, Emmy Sati would lose another.

Kevin McKee smiled down at the sleeping woman. Maybe afterwards, he could console her the way he wanted to. If not... then maybe Emmy Sati should be 'encouraged' to end her pain once and for all.

But what a waste that would be...

CHAPTER NINETEEN

With Duke's blessing, Emmy went to Princeton under the guise of seeking information about Max Neal and his connections there. The Dean was open and friendly and gave Emmy all the information he had—which was the same as the agency had already gathered.

They were sitting in the cafeteria when Emmy casually brought up Kevin McKee. "I understand he was the valedictorian in his year?"

"Oh yes, an outstanding student and a credit to this institution. He mentored the younger students, even, I believe he also helped out some of the poorer students financially."

"Really?"

"Oh yes."

Emmy sipped the coffee he had offered her. "Dean, I understand that secret societies are banned at Princeton? I only ask because I know sometimes there can be great financial benefits to membership in one of these groups."

The dean nodded. "You heard right, Agent Sati. We do not tolerate secret societies. Not that there aren't plenty of open societies, of course."

"Was Max Neal involved in any?"

"Not that I'm aware of."

"How about Martin Karlsson?"

The Dean's face grew sad. "Martin was another star student. Perhaps too easily led, but he had a kind heart. I was terribly sorry to hear about his death. Horrible. Just horrible." His eyes flicked to Emmy's forehead, still bruised. She had tried to cover it with makeup, but the dark black bruise was still vivid.

"Did Martin and Kevin know each other?"

The Dean shook his head. "I don't think so. There was a few years between them, not that Kevin didn't, and hasn't, stayed closely tied to the university."

"He still comes back to visit?"

"At least once a month."

That surprised her. "Once a month?"

The Dean smiled. "Yes, that is unusual for alumni, but Kevin has always been aware of his privilege, even I think sometimes embarrassed by it and wants to give back. As if serving his country wasn't enough."

"As the president's advisor?"

"And before, of course, in Iraq."

Wait... what? There was no record of military service in Kevin's file or in his public biography. Why would he hide it? Emmy simply smiled and nodded. "Of course."

The Dean glanced at his watch. "I hope you will forgive me, Agent, but I do have to get back to work." He stood, and Emmy shook his hand.

"Thank you for your time, sir. I do appreciate it."

"My pleasure. Feel free to wander around the campus, Agent, and if there's any other information you need, I shall tell my personal assistant to let you have it." His eyes drifted towards the bruises again, and he took her hand in both of his. "Thank you for your service, Agent. Take care of yourself."

The Dean was a sweetheart, Emmy decided, as she wandered around the campus. Her loyalty to Harvard didn't distract from the sheer joy of being back on a college campus. The beautiful buildings, the scurrying students heading between classes and seminars... if she decided to change direction, Emmy thought how much she would like to return to education, maybe take on a PhD.

She even talked to a few students, asking about afterschool clubs and societies, but now, in her mind, she wanted to explore Kevin McKee's expunged military career. She couldn't for the life of her understand why he would want it erased from his personal narrative.

Driving back to Washington, Emmy didn't notice the black sedan following her at first. It wasn't until she was crossing to Georgetown that it registered with her. She took an alternative route to her home, down side streets and even doubling back but the vehicle stayed resolutely behind her.

Shit.

Emmy gave up on going home and turned the car around, driving to the White House. As she turned onto Pennsylvania Avenue, the car tailing her peeled off and disappeared. "Bastard."

She had managed to catch half the registration and was processing it as Duke came to find her. "How'd it go?"

"Good. Nothing much on Max Neal that we didn't already know. Duke, close the door, would you?"

Duke looked surprised but did as she asked. Emmy hesitated a little. "Duke... did you know Kevin McKee served in the military?"

"No, he didn't."

"Not what the Dean of Princeton says. He told me McKee took a tour in Iraq."

Duke stared at her in disbelief. "What?"

Emmy nodded at her laptop. "I did a Google search, so it wouldn't show up on our system, but yeah. There's no public record of his service. Why?"

Duke shrugged. "I have no earthly idea."

"Something must have happened."

Emmy nodded. "So, I looked up Max Neal's military career. Turns out he served in the Middle East, too."

"Wait, wait, wait... Emmy, are you kidding me with this?"

"Duke, come on, if McKee served with Neal, that's a link."

Duke sighed, head in hands, thinking for a long minute. "Okay. So, we go to Lucas. Ask him why McKee's record is sealed and if we can find out in which unit he served. It still doesn't follow that they knew each other or that they're still in touch."

"Fair enough but I still think it's worth pursuing." Emmy debated telling Duke about her tail this morning but decided against it. She didn't want anyone fussing.

Duke didn't look happy, and he gazed at his friend. "You prepared for the shit storm if this all comes out?"

"I'm just doing my job, Duke." But she did wonder what Orin would think about her investigating one of his closest advisors.

When she saw him later, unfortunately only for a few stolen moments in the Oval, she didn't bring it up. Orin kissed her, then leaned his forehead against hers. "You're right about our bubble bursting," he said, but he smiled. "It's going to be a lot harder to sneak around here. Harder but not impossible."

Emmy, her arms around his waist, looked up at him. "Are you sure I'm worth the risk?"

"Don't ever ask me that again, my darling. You are worth everything to me."

CHAPTER TWENTY

Emmy and Orin knew that their affair would be difficult, and certainly not a regular thing, but after Orin's words of warning, Emmy was surprised how easy it was to sneak into the president's bedroom with Duke's help. "You realize you are absolutely my pimp now," she hissed at him as they walked through the passageway under the White House to the private residence.

Orin was waiting for her inside the bedroom, and going against protocol again, he locked the door. "Hey, beautiful." He bent his head to kiss her, and as their lips met, Emmy forgot about protocols, responsibility, and everything else.

"Hey yourself, Mr. President," she smiled, breathless as they broke apart.

Orin grinned, stroking her hair back behind her ears. "It's been a month, and every night I think of you."

Emmy nodded. "Me, too. It's been, I have to say, a weird time. Can we sit for a while? Just talk?"

"Of course, baby."

She felt a thrill go through her at the epithet, and as his hand closed around hers, leading her to the couches in front of the fire, she again felt that feeling of safety. Orin wrapped his arm around her shoulders and smiled down at her. "So, is this going to be a discussion on how reckless we're being?"

Emmy chuckled softly. "Well, we are, but that's beside the point. Orin, I'm going to recuse myself from your protection entirely."

He sighed but nodded. "I understand. God, I'm sorry."

"Don't be. It's my decision. I've spent the last week weighing everything up and I think..." she swallowed hard, "I think I need to tell Lucas Harper of our relationship. It isn't fair on Duke or Moxie or you. You have a country to run, and I'm a distraction."

"If Lucas knows... he could fire you."

She nodded. "He could, and maybe he should. I'll offer to resign."

"Wait... no." Orin stood up and paced, his handsome face creased with distress. "No, that isn't fair, Emmy, I got us into this."

"Excuse me, Mr. President, but I was a willing participant. I knew what I was doing, I knew that professionally, it was wrong."

"God." Orin shook his head. "Emmy, why should you have to—"

"Orin, come on. You're the president. Look, I can go into private security, be a consultant... there are plenty of options. Hell, I might even retrain as something else. Go back to school. I have a lot of options."

He narrowed his eyes at her. "And you've decided all this in only a month?"

Emmy almost lost her nerve. She had been practicing this speech for the last two days, but Orin was onto her. The thought of leaving the Secret Service was killing her, but she hated the sneaking around, and somehow, the thought of not being with Orin was even worse.

She'd argued with herself all month. You've slept with him, okay, but giving up your job? But Orin Bennett had brought her back to life. Since then, she'd felt a weight lift from her, and even Marge and her friends had noticed.

Orin sat back down beside her. "I can't give you up. I'm sorry if that makes me monumentally selfish, but it's the truth. I want you by my side, Emmy, as my partner, and I don't want to hide."

Emmy nodded and leaned over to kiss him. Something inside her wanted him to protest more, but what did she expect? He was the President of the United States, and she was just an agent.

And now his lover. "I don't want to talk anymore," she said softly, and Orin nodded, taking her in his arms.

"Emmy... what you're giving up for me, I can never repay."

He kissed her tenderly and then drew her to her feet. They walked to the bed and began to strip each other slowly. Emmy stroked his face, noticing he looked tired. "Are you okay?" She asked, and he nodded.

"Just this Ellis crap. It doesn't seem to be going away."

Emmy kissed him. "Let me be a distraction for just tonight. If Lucas lets me keep my job, I'll do everything in my power to help you. Hell, even if he doesn't, I'll—"

She was silenced by Orin's lips fierce against hers, and she kissed him back as he swept her into his arms and into bed. She could feel his cock, huge against her thigh, and she wrapped her legs around him. "Don't wait, baby."

Orin rolled a condom down over his cock and smiled down at her. "You are utterly intoxicating, Ms. Sati."

She grinned, and as he thrust into her, she tightened her arms around him, her lips against his as his cock plunged deep inside her welcoming, wet cunt. His fingers were on her clit, massaging it, teasing it until both her clit and her cunt were spasming with pleasure, and Emmy's body trembled with ecstasy.

They made love long into the early hours, talking in between, telling each other their hopes and dreams, leaving their careers outside of their discussion. In bed, they were just Emmy and Orin, and even when his mouth was sucking at her nipples, or his cock was plowing her into paradise, Emmy never felt less than his equal. She loved that about him.

At four a.m. Emmy slipped regretfully from his bed. "I have to go."

"I wish..."

She grinned at him. "What do you wish?"

"I wish you didn't have to go. I wish I could walk out of here holding your hand and tell the world that I'm in love with the most beautiful woman in the world." He stopped and laughed self-consciously. "I wish, I wish, I wish."

Emmy bent down and kissed him. "Get some sleep at least. You have to run the world in a few hours, Commander."

"Until next time?"

"Next time."

On the drive back to her home, Emmy wondered if she had gone a little crazy. She was really going to do this, really going to put her career on the line for this man. The full force of what she was about to do hit her hard, and she had to pull the car over to the side of the road to take some deep breaths. However she looked at it—she had thrown her career away for the sake of what? Nothing could ever come of their tryst. Orin could never openly date her, even if she wasn't in the Secret Service. She would be deemed unsuitable, not a politician or high-flying lawyer. She could see how the press would deride her—a lowly Agent—she could see it now. She'd be reduced to the president's fuck-buddy to the world.

And Zach... was she dishonoring his sacrifice by giving her career up? Her heart told her yes over and over again. Suddenly Emmy lost it, thumping the steering wheel and yelling Fuck! at the top of her voice.

For a moment, she closed her eyes, and then Emmy turned the car around and drove back to the field office. Lucas was talking to another agent as she entered the room, but when he saw her face, he knew something was wrong. He ushered her quickly into his office and shut the door.

"What? What is it, Em?"

Emmy took a deep breath in and met his gaze. "Lucas... I'm giving you my resignation. When you hear what I have to say, you may not want me to stay."

"Why?"

"Because I'm breaking every rule we have, Lucas. I've been derelict in my duty; I've lied to you and to the Service. Lucas... I'm sleeping with the president."

CHAPTER TWENTY-ONE

Lucas stared at Emmy for a moment, his face registering incomprehension. Then he grinned. "Very funny, Em. You got me there."

Emmy said nothing, her expression unchanging, and slowly, Lucas began to realize she wasn't joking. His eyes bugged, and his jaw actually dropped. "You are fucking kidding me?"

"No."

"What the fuck? Emmy..." He was obviously struggling to find the words, and Emmy braced herself for Lucas to lose his shit. She deserved it after all.

Lucas sat down heavily in his chair. "Sit down, Agent Sati."

Emmy sat and waited, her hands clasped together to stop them shaking. Lucas studied her.

"Now... God, I don't even know where to begin. You're telling me that you are in a sexual relationship with President Orin Bennett?"

"Yes, sir."

"How long?"

"A month, sir."

Lucas leaned back. "And you were both willing participants in this?"

"Yes, sir."

Lucas rubbed his forehead, trying to process what Emmy was telling him. "How often? Ugh, I hate having to ask that."

"Most nights, sir. At Camp David and at the White House."

"Were you on duty at the time?"

"No, sir, I was not."

"Well, that's something." Lucas shook his head at her. "Emmy, what the hell were you thinking? Have you feelings for Orin Bennett?"

"Yes, sir, I do."

"And he for you?"

"You would have to ask him, but he's indicated that—"

"Okay, okay." Lucas sighed. "Emmy... you realize the gravity of this situation?"

"I do, Lucas, that's why I came to you."

"After the fact."

Emmy felt her face burn. "Yes, sir."

Lucas got up and stared out the window for the longest time, and Emmy waited. She hated that she had disappointed him, her mentor and friend as well as her boss.

Finally, Lucas spoke. "I don't accept."

"Pardon me, sir?" Emmy was confused.

"Your resignation. I don't accept it. You'll be transferred. Obviously, your commitment to protecting the President is compromised, but I can't afford to lose one of my best agents for the sake of a few one-night stands. Even if it was with the President of the United States."

Emmy's fingernails were digging into her palms, and she felt a trickle of sweat trailing down her spine. "Lucas, I want you to know... I never meant for this to happen. I fought it for the longest time."

Lucas sat down heavily in his chair, staring at her unhappily. "Is this something to do with Zach's death? Did you come back too soon?"

"Lucas, I'm in love with Orin Bennett and he with me." There it was—out in the open. Lucas sighed and rubbed his eyes.

"God, Emmy."

"I know."

They sat in silence for a while. "You must have had help sneaking around the White House."

"Yes, sir."

"Care to share names?"

"No, sir."

Lucas's mouth twitched. "Good girl," he said quietly. He leaned forward on his desk. "You'll be assigned off the detail, but still with access, so to speak. I'll tell my superiors that you've shown an aptitude for investigation and wished to be reassigned so you can concentrate on the threats to the president. That, at least, will be true." He smiled at her. "Thank you, Emmy. Really, I had no idea and you could have kept this secret for months. I appreciate your honesty."

Emmy walked out of Lucas's office and went to her own. Duke was in there, and he looked surprised to see her. "Hey, I didn't think you were on today."

She closed the door behind her. "Duke... I just told Lucas."

"What the hell?" Duke looked alarmed, but she waved him down.

"I didn't tell him anything about you, don't worry. But he knows about me and the president."

"And Lucas makes five." Duke sat back in his chair, shaking his head. "In all honesty, Em, how do you and Bennett expect to keep this to yourselves?"

"As long as we can. Until things are... resolved one way or the other."

She hated the pitying look she could see in Duke's eyes. "Baby girl... you know how this is going to end. Is it all worth it?"

Emmy met his gaze steadily and nodded. "Yes, Duke... he is."

Later that morning, Orin was in the Oval with Moxie, Kevin, and Issa, discussing a speech Orin was to give to a room full of business leaders later in the week. As Moxie spoke, detailing the reasons for the speech, Orin found his mind drifting yet again. In this morning's security briefing, Lucas Harper had told him that Max Neal had gone so far underground that it was hard to believe they'd ever find him.

"Of course, this means we're having to change your security arrangements. One of the reasons, anyway."

Orin had looked up at that, saw the look in Lucas's eyes, and nodded. "Emmy told me that she'd spoken to you."

"Your relationship is none of my business, sir—"

"—no."

"—but my agent's welfare is. I hope you have both considered the implications of your continued, um, assignations."

Orin couldn't hide his grin then. "Assignations, Lucas?"

To his credit, Lucas smiled. "Sorry, sir. I'm just looking out for my agent."

As he turned to go, Orin called him back. "Lucas... thank you for not firing Emmy. She deserves better."

"Yes, sir. She does."

Whether Lucas meant that as a reprimand or not, Orin took it to heart. When, that evening, Emmy came to the Lincoln Bedroom, he kissed her, then searched her eyes. "Are you okay?"

"Sure. Why? Something happen?"

Orin smiled down at her. "Just wondering. Lucas told me he knew today."

"Ah."

"He's not giving you a hard time, is he?"

Emmy grinned. "No. I kind of wish he was, but no, he's been very fair."

"So, you're an investigating agent now?"

"Just like Cagney. Or Lacey. Take your pick."

Orin laughed. "Are you even old enough to know who Cagney and Lacey were?"

"Wash your mouth out, Bennett. Cagney and Lacey are my heroines. Now, drop trou."

Orin busted up. "You see? No one can make me laugh like you, Emerson Sati. No one makes me feel this much—"

"—what?"

"Joy." He said it simply but with a depth of emotion that made Emmy's heart flip.

"I love you so much," she said. "Perhaps even more than I loved Zach... no, that's wrong. I love you differently. With Zach, I always felt... like a giggly teenager and that was good, exactly what I needed right then in my life. I will always love and thank him for that. But with you—" She stroked his face. "I feel like a woman. Someone who went through the worst and came out—and now sees love in a totally different way. I know it isn't always easy and laid back and uncomplicated."

Orin's mouth was on hers then, and they forgot all about talking as they stripped each other's clothes off and lay down on the bed.

Orin stroked his hand down her body, cupping her breasts. "Curvy Goddess."

Emmy grinned. "Indian blood. No skinny girls in my family."

"Good. Do you see them often?"

She shook her head. "Not for many years now; none of us keep in touch. We were never close knit to begin with. It wasn't until Zach that I realized what a family could be. Now my neighbor Marge and my agency brethren are my family. Oh, and Zach's cousin from Australia."

"I heard about him. Moxie said he was the spitting image of Zach. That must have been difficult."

"It was, I admit. But in a strange way, he's helped me." She rested her chin on his chest, smiling up at him. "What about you?"

"Only child. Parents died a few years ago. Like you, my family is constructed out of the people closest to me. Moxie, Peyton, Charlie."

Emmy chewed her lip. "Kevin?"

"And Kevin and Issa, too. And now you, Emmy. I can't imagine my life without you."

"Nor I, you."

Orin stroked her hair back behind her ears, gazing at her with so much love that Emmy forgot everything else. He gently pushed her onto her back and began to make love to her. Emmy savored every moment, every touch, as he thrust into her, and they began to move together. Orin didn't neglect any part of her body as he kissed, caressed, and tasted her, sucking on her nipples until they were rock hard, stroking her belly until it quivered under his touch.

It was almost three o'clock before they finally fell asleep, but Emmy's dreams were wracked with torment, and when she woke, gasping and sobbing, Orin took her in his arms. "What is it, my love? What is it?"

Emmy struggled to catch her breath then slumped against him. "I don't know why... but I don't want you to give that speech. Don't give the speech..."

CHAPTER TWENTY-TWO

"I'm sorry, baby, but I can't cancel the speech. Everything's planned. People have come in from—"

"It's okay, Orin, really. I was being—I just had a bad dream, and I was being stupid. I'm sorry." Emmy was back at home now, later in the afternoon, and Orin had called her twice already. "I'm sorry I put you through that."

"Through what? You had a bad dream is all. I'm sure we'll both have our share during our life together."

She smiled down the phone. "Our life together."

"You bet your sweet ass."

She chuckled. "Really, is that any sort of language for the Oval Office?"

"Well, I put it to the Senate and they decided that yes, you have a sweet ass."

"You're a terrible President."

Orin laughed. "I know, I know. Listen. The speech is three days away, and it's locked. That almost never happens. Kevin had really knocked it out of the park on this one."

Emmy bit her lip. "Good. I'm glad."

"You okay?"

Orin must have picked up on the hesitation in her voice. "Of course."

"Look, the State Dinner tonight... I want you to know that if I had my way, you'd be there right next to me."

"We have to be realistic, darling... oh, Orin, someone's banging on my door. I have to go."

"Tomorrow then?"

"Tomorrow."

Emmy pulled open her front door and her heart failed. Kevin McKee smiled at her—a smile that didn't reach his eyes—and chuckled. "You look like you've seen a ghost, Emmy. May I come in?"

Numbly she stood aside and let him in, glancing around for any potential weapons she could use if he attacked her. Her service pistol was in the bedroom. She was quick, but Kevin was a big guy.

He smiled at her. "I'm sorry to intrude but I wanted to talk to you about something."

She nodded stiffly. "Can I get you a drink?"

"Coffee would be great, thanks." He looked around her apartment. "Your boyfriend live here, too?"

None of your damn business. "No. I only have instant coffee, I'm afraid."

"Love the stuff."

She went into the kitchen, her nerves tingling and on edge as she filled the kettle. Turning toward the cupboard, she yelped in alarm. Kevin was standing directly behind her.

"Sorry, sorry, I should have said something."

His hand was on her face and Emmy stepped backward. Kevin smiled. "My apologies again, I didn't mean to scare you, lovely Emmy."

Ok, this was just getting weird. "So," he said, heaving himself onto her kitchen counter, his body language casual, friendly, "I hear you've been up at Princeton asking questions. Anything I can help you with?"

Careful now, careful. "I was. Your name came up, naturally, given what you achieved there, but I was there to ask about Max Neal."

Kevin nodded slowly. "Max matriculated there after me, but I did meet him a couple of times. I found him—unimpressive."

"In what way?"

"He had all the fire and bluster of a militant—and none of the conviction. Emmy, can I be honest?"

"Please." She handed him a cup of coffee, and he thanked her.

"In my opinion—the Secret Service is placing way too much faith in Max Neal. From what I know, I simply don't think he has the organization, money, or connections to launch an assault on the president."

Emmy took this in. Instead of directly answering him, she decided to go another way. "I'm more interested in his military record. I know he served." She met Kevin's gaze. "I'm wondering if something happened to him over there, to make him this—angry. So angry he could blow up a gymnasium full of kids."

Kevin held her gaze steadily. "He was always that angry, Emmy. Some people just do… bad things."

Emmy sipped her coffee. "Have you ever done a bad thing, Kevin?"

There was a silence then he smiled. "Are you flirting with me, Agent Sati?"

Ugh. But she smiled. "No, just joking around. Kevin, why did you come here?"

His smile faded. "Emmy, I came here to warn you."

Her adrenaline spiked as Kevin jumped off the counter. "As a friend… your late-night visits to the Lincoln bedroom…"

Oh fuck. Emmy kept her face blank. "I'm sorry?"

Kevin smiled. "I'm just saying… people know—and people who aren't the friends of the president know. I just wanted you to be prepared if anything should happen."

"So, it's a friendly warning?" She knew exactly what this was. Stop sticking your nose in my business or I'll leak you're fucking the President. He had her there. Bastard.

Kevin touched her face again, and she tried not to flinch. "God, you're beautiful. I can see why he fell for you, Emmy. I just want you both to be happy." He checked his watch. "Damn, I have to get back for the State Dinner. Will you be working it?"

He made her sound like a hooker touting for Johns. "No, I'm off duty tonight. I'll be at the speech on Friday."

"Well, I'll see you then. Thanks for the coffee." And he was gone.

Emmy closed the door after him and locked it. Creep. How he had known she was looking into his military record she didn't know, but it wasn't as if she had found anything. All the doors she'd tried in the last month had been slammed in her face. What the hell was Kevin McKee hiding?

She felt uneasy in her own home after McKee's visit, and tucking her service pistol in her waistband, she went across the hall to see Marge and spent the evening with her neighbor. At midnight, she went home, making sure all the doors and windows were locked, and slipped her gun under her pillow. Her tension only eased when her phone bleeped with a message.

Miss you being beside me. I love you. O.

CHAPTER TWENTY-THREE

The ballroom at the Kennedy Center was packed for the president's speech on Friday night. Emmy, Duke, and a dozen other agents were milling around, checking all the security arrangements which had been in place for weeks.

Backstage, Lucas and a number of other agents were waiting for the president to arrive and when he did, Orin greeted them. "Hey, fellas. How's it looking, Lucas?"

As they walked through the hallways, Orin caught sight of Emmy at the far end of the corridor. She had on a long, white figure-hugging dress, her long hair down, and Orin's heart nearly stopped. *The woman I love.* He wanted to yell it out, scream it out, and take her in his arms in front of the audience, the press, the world. *Fuck what they thought.*

She turned and caught his eye and smiled. Orin touched his heart, subtle but meaningful, before he was escorted to the stage.

Emmy took up her post at the side of the stage, her eyes raking the audience as Orin began to speak. The feeling that something would happen tonight had returned, and she had been unable to sleep last night because of it. She had gone over every detail of the security plan that night, even checking places that the team had gone over again and again.

Orin's voice was warm and friendly, and she wanted to listen to what he was saying but something was nagging at her. She kept Kevin McKee in her sights as well as the gathered audience of invited guests. Her eyes swept over every single person—and locked on one man in particular. He was fairly innocuous—white, middle-aged, and bearded, sitting with someone Emmy vaguely recognized from the pages of a magazine. The reason he piqued her interest was because of the way he was looking at McKee and then the president.

Was he waiting for a signal?

The rest of the speech went off without incident, however, and it wasn't until the audience were standing and applauding that Emmy saw him reach into his pocket. Her senses up, the room began to go into slow motion as she saw the glint of something in his hand.

No. No way.

Emmy threw herself at Orin just as her whole world exploded in pain.

Bedlam. Orin was dragged off the stage by Lucas and Duke just as the gunshots rang out, but all he could see was his love, his Emmy, prone on the floor, eyes closed, her white dress covered in blood. He fought with his detail to get to her, but they dragged him away—a pretty impressive feat—as he screamed Emmy's name.

As Lucas forced him into the car and they sped away, Orin turned wild eyes to the security chief. "Tell me she's okay, tell me she's okay!"

Lucas looked shell shocked and pale. "Mr. President, we have to get you back to the White House."

Orin exploded, his terror for his lover overwhelming everything. "Turn the fucking car around! Now!"

"No, sir. We cannot do that."

"That's an order from your Commander-in-Chief!"

"No, sir. We are going back to the White House." Lucas's voice was strong, and he fixed Orin with a stare that said "I know. I know you're in pain, but this is how it is."

Orin slumped back into his seat with a moan. "At least get someone on the phone. I want to know how she is, right now."

Lucas gave a stiff nod, obviously relieved Orin was obeying him. He called Duke. "What's happening?"

The paramedics were there almost immediately. Duke directed them to Emmy's prone figure on the dais, his mind whirling. What the hell just happened? The top brass had been secured, the gunman subdued and arrested, the ballroom cleared out, and now Duke, his throat closing, went to his stricken friend.

She was paler than he had ever seen her, lying in a pool of blood. The bullet had smashed into her abdomen and now her white dress was soaked red. The paramedics were trying to get a response out of her.

"Emmy? Emmy, if you can hear me, squeeze my hand." The paramedic waited then shook her head. "Nothing. Unresponsive."

"No exit wound. We have to get her to the hospital right now."

Duke finally found his voice as his phone rang. Lucas. "They're rushing her to hospital now, GW. She took a slug in the gut, Lucas... there's so much blood, and she's not responding to us."

He hardly heard Lucas's reply as he walked with the gurney to the ambulance. "I'll call you when we get there."

"I want to go to the hospital right now," Orin told his staff as the Secret Service gathered them in the Oval. "No arguments."

He looked at Moxie, who shook her head slightly in warning at him, but Orin was too upset to care.

"The rest of you should know. Agent Sati and myself are in a serious relationship. I love her. And to think that she..." His voice broke down, and Peyton came to put her arm around him.

"Look, let's sit. If they're taking Emmy to hospital, she'll be in surgery a while. Orin, sit, take a breath and we'll figure out what to do from here."

Emmy opened her eyes and took a long painful breath in. All she could see was ceiling tiles and quick flashes of people looking down on her. It was disorientating. "Orin?"

Duke's face, drawn and pale came into view. "Baby girl, you're awake. Thank God."

"Is Orin okay?"

Duke nodded. "The president is fine, Em. You saved his life."

Emmy relaxed, but as her adrenaline seeped away, the pain got worse. "Shit. What happened, Duke? Fuck, that hurts..."

Duke smiled despite himself. "You've been shot, doofus." His smile faded, and he held her hand tightly. "It's bad, Em. They're going to take you to surgery any minute. You promise me now... you fight, okay?"

She nodded.

"Say it aloud, Em." Duke's voice broke, and she tried to smile at him.

"I promise. He's really okay?"

A tear dropped down Duke's cheek. "He really is, kiddo. And if it helps, we had to drag him away from you."

Emmy smiled, then another face hovered into view. "We're going to take you to surgery now, Emerson, and get that bullet out of you."

In a matter of minutes, Emmy was in theater and as she was put under, she wondered if she would ever wake up, but was happy knowing that even if she died, the man she loved was alive.

I love you, Orin Bennett... and she was out.

CHAPTER TWENTY-FOUR

Orin Bennett stood at the lectern in the White House press room and waited for the media to settle down. It had been a week since the shooting, a week since his darling love, his Emmy, had taken that bullet for him.

Three days since the press had found out about his and Emmy's relationship—Kevin McKee's parting gift before he was arrested for conspiracy in the attempted murder of the president.

Two days since Emmy's research had finally come up with the goods on Max Neal and Kevin McKee's shared history and friendship.

One day since Emmy had finally woken up from a coma. They'd operated on her and removed the bullet, but she lost so much blood that it was touch and go.

When finally, Lucas Harper had allowed Orin to go to the hospital, he hadn't left her side. He told his team not to interfere with the running of the hospital, but he was staying by Emmy's side. The press had caught wind of it, of course, and the media had been full of speculation until Kevin confirmed it all in the last moments of his job.

Now, Orin stood in front of the press to make the most important statement of his political life. "Thanks for coming, ladies and gentlemen. I'll be making a short statement then I'll take any questions you might have."

He cleared his throat and stood tall, his hands on the podium. "A week ago, my life was saved from an assassin's bullet by an exemplary member of the US Secret Service. Her name is Emerson Sati. Emmy. Emmy is her name, and she is not only a national hero, she is the woman I love. A few days ago, former Communications Director Kevin McKee was arrested for conspiracy based on Emmy's investigation into the threats made against me. Before that, he leaked to the press details of my relationship with Emerson Sati."

Orin, his face set and grim, looked at every member of the press corps. "And some of you have tried to destroy Agent Sati's character based on gossip and rumor. You know who you are. Shame on you. Shame on you. That young woman is a hero. You have painted her as a gold digging unprofessional whore. Shame on you. So here, for the record, is the true story, not that it is in any way your business."

Orin could see Moxie out of the corner, looking worried about what he was going to say but he had no fucks left to give now.

"I fell in love with Emmy Sati the moment I saw her. Over the course of many weeks, we had the opportunity to talk, and it became clear that a mutual attraction existed between us. A month ago, we began a discreet sexual relationship. Agent Sati recused herself, ironically, from my protection, and concentrated on investigating the threats against me, and the connection to the bombing at the school in Maryland. Agent Sati also informed her superiors of the relationship and offered her resignation which was not accepted by Lucas Harper—and I would not be alive today if he had."

Orin paused. "Over the past few weeks I've been given advice from many sources about who I should love, who they should be, what the American public will accept. I say to you now... last night I asked Emerson Sati to be my wife. Your First Lady. And if you think that an American heroine is not fit to be First Lady... then by all means, vote me out of office in three and a half years'-time. Now I'll take your questions."

Across town, in George Washington Hospital, Marge and Tim were whooping with delight at the president's words as Emmy looked on, blushing furiously and smiling. Orin's words were a shot of pure morphine to her aching body.

Marge nudged her. "Well? Come on, don't leave us in suspense. What did you say?"

Emmy's eyes shone. "I said yes, of course," she said softly and groaned as Marge hugged her.

"Whoops, sorry Moo. Oh, Moo... First Lady..."

"Damn, you'll be too fancy for the likes of us now." Tim grinned at her, and she was happy to see no rancor or recrimination in his eyes.

"I will be," she sniffed haughtily. "In fact, who are you people? How did you get in?" She giggled as they both stuck out their tongues at her—Marge and Tim were quite the double act these days. Tim nodded wisely.

"Listen... do they knowing about the chronic farting?"

"And the snoring. Don't forget the snoring."

"The kleptomania," Tim added, and Marge cackled.

"The weird fetish magazines."

Emmy chuckled. "You mean National Geographic?"

"Those ones."

Emmy listened to their teasing but before long, she found herself falling asleep again. When she woke, Tim and Marge had left, and next to her, his fingers linked in hers, was her fiancé. Her Orin. The man she loved.

"Hey you."

He looked up and his eyes lit up. "Hey, beautiful. How are you feeling?"

"So much better after seeing your press conference. You really gave it to them."

"They deserved it." He stroked her face. "Emerson Sati, have you any idea how much I love you?"

"At least as much as I love you, Mr. President."

Orin grinned. "Say the words again to me, Emmy, so I can start to believe my good fortune. Will you marry me?"

Emmy smiled at him. "Yes, Orin Bennett, I will marry you."

"I just had to be sure." He leaned his forehead against hers. "I'm the most selfish man on the planet because I'm asking you to give up so much—so, so much—and I feel like I'm reaping all the rewards."

"Nah. I nabbed the President of the United States. I won the lottery." She giggled to show she was just kidding, and Orin laughed.

"Seriously," he said, "it's going to be a rough ride from here on in. Sure you want to do it?"

"With you? Hell yes. Let's make a difference." She winced and shifted a little, pressing the meds button to release a shot of morphine. "Orin... tell me again about Kevin McKee. I'm sure I didn't take it all in the other day."

"You were right. He served with Max Neal in Iraq. What we've found out from the military is that Kevin and Max were involved in some of stand-off with a bunch of Iraqi teenagers. Things went south. Long story short, Neal took the fall for Kevin, big time. Kevin got his record sealed—strange what old family money can do—and yeah, he fooled us all."

"Why did he want you dead?"

Orin shook his head. "He didn't. I was the favor Max Neal called in or he would have gone public. Kevin told the agency that he was looking for Neal, too, that if he found him first, Neal would have gotten the bullet." Orin sighed, smoothing a hand over her forehead. "But he sent those men to kill you and Martin Karlsson. He thought Max Neal had told Karlsson about the incident in Iraq—and Karlsson had told you."

"God..." Emmy felt sick. She'd let that man into her apartment. Orin shook his head.

"Kevin admitted he went to your apartment to kill you but couldn't do it."

"He just gave me a warning. Stupid man. If anything, that made me more determined to find out about him." Emmy sighed. "So, really, it had very little to do with the Ellis case?"

"Yup. But you paid the price, darling, and I'm so sorry."

"Hey," Emmy said with a soft smile. "I'm going to be fine, Orin. I would take that bullet over and over again for you, you know that."

Orin winced and placed his hand over her wounded belly. "Never again. Never." He kissed her gently. "From now on, Emmy, good things only, I swear. Having said that, we may have a fight on our hands."

Emmy grinned at him. "So what else is new?"

CHAPTER TWENTY-FIVE

One month later...

There was a field of press waiting for Emmy to leave the hospital, and she felt a wave of nerves flood her. Moxie and Issa had drilled her on the questions she would face, and Emmy realized this was her life now. She glanced up at Orin with panic in her eyes, but he smiled at her and took her hand.

"Don't worry, baby," he said in a low voice. "This will be easy."

She appreciated the lie but knew this was only the first challenge. The hospital insisted that she leave in a wheelchair as per hospital policy, and Orin told them in no uncertain terms that he would be the one pushing the wheelchair.

To his astonishment, and to Emmy's, Moxie had been supportive. "Good, that's good. If we're really going to do this, then we need to make sure we're all in. And the visuals will be good, too." She looked apologetically at Emmy. "Sorry, Em, but from now on, that will always be a consideration."

"I know." But her stomach still roiled with nerves.

She had already been freaked out by the fact that Lucas was no longer her boss but her protector. They'd both been sad the day she had officially quit her job at the agency.

"But, Lucas, you can bet I'll use my position to champion the agency."

Lucas had smiled at her. "I know you will, Em."

"I'm so sorry for embarrassing you, for letting you down."

He gaped at her. "You did no such thing, Emerson Sati. You saved the life of the President of the United States. Your investigative work helped bring a traitor to justice. You are a credit to the Service."

"Except the whole sleeping with the president thing." But she smiled at his words. "Thank you, Lucas. For everything. For how you treated me after Zach, for mentoring me."

Now, as Orin pushed her wheelchair out of the doors of the hospital, Emmy took a deep breath in. Orin bent down and kissed her cheek. "I love you," he murmured, "more than anything.

Emmy smiled up at him, told him she loved him, and then turned to face her future...

The End

CPSIA information can be obtained
at www.ICGtesting.com
Printed in the USA
BVHW041606080221
599639BV00010B/767